T0114652

Alex Revere and Brady's Missing Superbowl Jersey

CHRIS JENKINS

BALBOA.PRESS
A DIVISION OF HAY HOUSE

Balboa Press books may be ordered through booksellers or by contacting:

Balboa Press
A Division of Hay House
1663 Liberty Drive
Bloomington, IN 47403
www.balboapress.com
844-682-1282

Print information available on the last page.

ISBN: 979-8-7652-2843-2 (sc)
ISBN: 979-8-7652-2844-9 (e)

Balboa Press rev. date: 08/01/2022

This book is dedicated to the greatest NFL quarterback who has ever lived on this planet—the one and only Patriot who's won nine AFC Championship titles, six Super Bowl rings, and four Super Bowl MVP awards. There are no other quarterbacks in history who have achieved these accomplishments. However, I apologize for the unique, divine, and blessed Super Bowl jersey that was stolen in February of 2017 after your miraculous comeback in Super Bowl 51 against the Atlanta Falcons.

I watched every second of that game and was honored to say, "Don't ever count Brady out!" We patiently waited to see the day you'd achieve six rings and become a legend like the great Michael Jordan, although in many eyes you're already a legend. That number 12 Super Bowl jersey you wore as you achieved your fifth ring had to be precious to you. You made history wearing that jersey.

What other NFL quarterback has four Super Bowl MVP awards? None! What quarterback has forced the Super Bowl to go into overtime? What other NFL quarterback has six Super Bowl victories? Your number 12 Patriot jersey is unique, blessed, and mystical. So I wrote this story to show the world and to keep your jersey alive *forever*!

CONTENTS

ONE

Stressed and Depressed

Thursday, September 14, 2017

ALEX SAT IN THE REAR OF THE CLASSROOM, DAYDREAMING. THE senior high school student was filled with misery and disappointment. His English teacher Ms. Bonae was monitoring him from her desk. Alex had lost concentration since the deaths of his mother and father. He was disregarding his classwork and repudiating school. He was making irrational decisions and was no longer determined to be valedictorian. The teachers had no idea why Alex was so discouraged, though his grades informed them something was wrong. There had been a time when Alex Revere's grades were the best of his class and unexceptionable. Since school had begun a month ago, however, Alex had failed to impress his English teacher.

The last bell rang extremely loudly, echoing around the high school campus. The hallways were immediately filled with young adults aged fourteen to eighteen, and Alex stood from his light-brown desk, grabbed his backpack, and headed for the door. As the queue of teenagers was exiting the classroom, his English teacher called out to him.

"Mr. Alex Revere! I need to have a word with you before you go," Ms. Bonae shouted, her tone serious.

Alex paused, turned around, and approached the teacher's desk. He looked deeply into her pretty brown eyes. "What is it Ms. Bonae?"

The beautiful young Spanish lady remained seated in her black chair behind the desk. With her head down, she glanced over the rim of her eyeglasses at Alex. "It's your grades, young man. Alex, if you don't get your grades together, you won't be graduating with honors. Also, football will no longer be an option," she said querulously.

"I understand, Ms. Bonae," Alex replied sympathetically.

"I mean, come on, Alex. The school year has just begun, and you're already slacking. But according to your freshman, sophomore, and junior year transcripts, you were a straight-A student. I mean … is everything all right at home?" she asked, concerned.

Alex contemplated disclosing his personal information involving his family. He then took a deep breath while gazing into her eyes. "No, not really. My mother and father just died in a car crash a couple months ago. That is what really has me off balance," he said truthfully.

"Aww, Alex! I am so, so sorry to hear that," his teacher replied apologetically.

He replied nonchalantly. "Yeah. That's what everybody says. But honestly … very few people can relate and understand." He paused for a moment to see if she had anything else to say. Once he realized she didn't have a response, he took the initiative to conclude the conversation. "Well, Ms. Bonae, I have to get going to football practice. I will do my best to get my grades together," he said plainly.

Ms. Bonae didn't say anything as he walked toward the door. The only thing she could do was shake her head. Of course she knew of Alex's family. The entire Revere family were philanthropists and prominent in Detroit, practically equivalent to the Bushes.

As the six-foot-four senior walked out of the classroom, he saw his girlfriend, Alicia. She was headed his way, looking for him. "Hey, baby," she said as she approached him.

"Hey there, Alicia." Alex smiled and gave her a long, passionate hug. He genuinely loved and cared about the beautiful sixteen-year-old junior. The two of them had been dating for several years, since middle school.

Alicia was only five foot seven and weighed 137 pounds. Her extremely long hair hung down near the middle of her back. After giving Alex a hug, she noticed the new tattoo on Alex's skin. "When did you get the new tattoo?" she asked curiously. He glanced down at the greenish-colored ink that read:

R.I.P. Anna and Bob
Forever Love Mom and Dad

Uniquely, both of his parents' names were palindromes. It didn't matter if you read their names backward or forward, they would still be the same.

"I got this yesterday. I had to get something in remembrance of my parents," he said. The couple held hands as they walked down the high school hallway.

"And what were you doing in there? Let me guess. Another teacher giving you a lecture again," said Alicia knowingly.

"Yep!" he replied. The hallway was predominantly empty now. Many of the students had already departed the school and gone home or to their next destination.

"Do you have football practice today?" she asked rhetorically.

Alex looked at Alicia. "Yes. You know I do. Why do you ask?"

"Because tomorrow is your birthday … And I was hoping that maybe you could spend tonight at my house," she said, smiling.

They were standing face to face near the football stadium.

"What about your parents?" he asked.

"They're leaving tonight. They won't be back until Sunday morning."

"And your little brother?"

"I gave him twenty dollars. I'm sure he'll keep his mouth closed for that much," she said.

Alex laughed at the truthful comment. "Are you sure he's not going to tell your parents on us?"

"I'm positive! Besides, he's only six. That's the most money he's ever had in his whole life."

"All right, baby. I'll be there as soon as football practice is over," he replied, smiling.

"Great! I'll be waiting," she said.

Alicia kissed Alex on the lips and walked away flamboyantly. He was mesmerized by her sexy body, flawless complexion, and unique walk. Once she was out of sight, he headed toward the bleachers where the other players were.

Being the backup quarterback wasn't a position to be proud about. Although he hoped to be starting soon, Alex really didn't care anymore. He loved the Fort Miner Fireballs and every player on the team—except for the starting quarterback. It was mostly because the senior quarterback was a much better passer than he was. Alex's completion percentage had been less than 40 percent for the last two years. Ultimately, he couldn't compete with the starting quarterback, whose completion percentage was 68 percent.

As Alex walked over to the bleachers, his friend James said, "What's up, Alex?"

"Nothing much. The sky. That's all I see," replied Alex, unenthused.

James was the starting running back on their team. The young, dark-skinned kid could run like a cheetah on steroids. The depressed expression on Alex's face must have shown because James then said,

"Alex, you have to cheer up and pull yourself together, man. Instead of stressing about your parents, make them proud," said James, in an inspirational way.

Another player on the bleachers next to James then said, "Yeah, Alex. My dad died last year too, man. Ever since then, I take all of my pain and frustration, put it into the football, and release it," said Cody. Cody was the starting wide receiver. Alex admired him a lot, even though they were the same age.

Cody and James were both a positive influence on Alex. He listened attentively while the two players gave him their advice. "That's just something to think about," added James.

"I'm going to get myself together soon. It's just … you guys are starting players in every game. So you both get the chance to prove yourself. Coach Parker acts like he has something against me because I'm white," said Alex seriously.

James smiled at the ridiculous comment. "Don't be ridiculous, Alex! Coach Parker is married to a white lady," said James.

"And has three kids with her," added Cody quickly.

"So I know he's not a racist. You just have to get back to being focused, Alex. Then he'll put you back in the game," said James.

A few seconds later, they all heard a loud whistle blow. The three of them turned and looked, seeing Coach Parker blowing the whistle. "All right, Fireballs! Let's get on this field and get this practice started. We have a third game coming up tomorrow," shouted the coach.

"Yeah, we do need to practice! We've already lost our first two games," said Cody.

"Really!" blurted out Alex.

"Yeah, Alex. Where've you been?" said James.

Cody and James stood up and ran toward the football field. Alex grabbed his backpack and started walking away. Discouraged and depressed, he decided to leave after the conversation with the two starting players. As he was departing, Coach Parker yelled out for him. "Hey, Alex!" Alex glanced back at the coach. "Come here for a minute," Coach Parker added.

Alex took a deep breath, turned around, and walked over to the coach. As he approached, Coach Parker said, "Listen, Alex! The starting quarterback is leaving!"

"Who? Shawn?" replied, Alex, dumbfounded.

"Yes, Shawn. His parents are moving to Florida. Tomorrow will be his last game playing with us. The team is going to need you to step up to the position and lead. Are you ready for that?" asked Coach Parker intently.

Alex contemplated the question before he said, "Yeah, coach! No! I mean … I don't know, coach."

"Look here, kid. You have two days to meditate on it. Go home, gather your thoughts, and let me know Saturday, all right?" said the coach.

Alex smiled at the tall black man then said, "All right." The two shook hands, and Alex departed from the football field. He walked to the parking lot and entered his 2016 red Corvette Stingray.

Alex had received $500,000 from his parents' life insurance policy, due to the fact he was their only child. Besides the Corvette, Alex really hadn't spent much of the money. He still had over $400,000 left in his savings account. Alex ignited the engine of the luxurious Chevy, placed the car in drive, and zoomed out of the school's parking lot.

It didn't take him long to arrive at his grandmother's house. Since the death of his parents, he'd had the choice of several different relatives to go reside with. He knew everybody was welcoming him in with greedy intentions. He'd chosen to go live with the person he knew would welcome him out of sincere love and sympathy: his maternal grandmother.

Alex walked into the home and saw his grandmother cooking dinner in the kitchen. She glanced at the door and gazed into his eyes as he entered. "Good afternoon, Granny!" said Alex.

"Oh, hey there, Alexander! How was your day at school, sweetheart?" she asked genuinely.

"Same old stuff as always," he replied.

She quit stirring the pot and placed it on a different burner to avoid it boiling. She exited the kitchen and walked to the living room where Alex was standing. "Have a seat, Alex," she said.

He followed his grandmother's instruction without debate. "What is it now, Grandma?" he asked.

She wiped her hands with a damp washcloth before setting it on the coffee table. "Your teacher called me about your grades. Baby, you have to remain focused," she said softly. "Look at me, Alex!"

He lifted his head, and gave her the eye contact she desired. "You used to be a straight-A student. That's the Alex I want to see. It's only the second month of school, and you're not doing your homework or completing assignments *already*," she said.

"Grandma, I'm going through a lot, and you know it," he replied.

"Listen, Alex, and you listen to me good! Your mother and father were doctors. They weren't some low-grade, worthless parents who would've raised you wrong. They both graduated with a 4.0 average and went to college at Georgetown in Washington, DC Don't you want to make them proud if they're looking down on you?" she asked.

"Yeah, Granny, I do!" said Alex.

"Well, get it together so you can graduate with that 4.0 and not a 2.0!" she said.

He smiled. "OK, Grandma, I will!" he said.

"All right Alex! Don't make me look bad," she reminded him.

"I promise I won't," he replied.

Alex stood and gave his grandmother a nice, warm hug. After they'd embraced one another, he headed upstairs to his room. On his way, she shouted up to him, "Your birthday present is on your bed! I decided to give it to you a day early!"

"OK, Granny!" Alex replied. When he entered his room, he saw a box wrapped in red, white, and blue paper with a big American flag on top of it. *Great! More clothes for my birthday*, he grumbled in his mind

Alex walked over to his bed and sat on the edge. He picked up the box and shook it up, then tossed it in his closet on the floor. Alex opened his backpack and pulled out his textbooks and a pencil and began doing his calculus homework. It didn't take him long to complete it. After he'd finished, he placed it in a red folder. He reached in his backpack again to grab more unfinished work from several different classes. Alex put the pencil to the assignments and began completing the work. Once he was done, he glanced up at the clock on the wall.

Nine twenty-eight?! There is no way I've been doing school work for almost five hours, he thought. He reached over to his nightstand, grabbed his Galaxy cell phone, and looked at the screen. *Forty-four missed calls?! Oh God! Alicia is gonna to be pissed!*

Without further delay, he dialed his girlfriend's phone number. When she answered, he could tell she was upset by the sound of her voice. After giving her his genuine explanation, though, she calmed down.

"Well, how long before you get here?" she asked.

"After I gather my clothes and things, I'll be on my way," said Alex.

"All right then, baby! I love you," she said.

"Love you too," he replied, hanging up. Alex packed up right away. He told his grandma he was spending the night at Alicia's house and then departed.

TWO

The Special Missing Super Bowl Jersey

Friday, September 15, 2017

ALEX WOKE UP IN BED NEXT TO ALICIA AND EXAMINED HIS CELL phone—7:08 a.m. He tapped his girlfriend's shoulder to wake her up.

"What, Alex? I'm tired!" she mumbled from under the blankets.

"We have to get ready for school," he said.

"My parents are gone. Me and my little brother aren't going to school," she replied.

"Well, I'm going, baby," he said.

"Come on, *Alex*! Please don't go. Stay here with me," she said.

"I can't, babe! I promised my grandmother I'd get serious about my grades and schoolwork," Alex replied.

"What's one day going to hurt?" she asked.

Alex paused and thought about it. "Nah! I'm going to school," he finally said.

Alicia rolled over in the bed. "Well, happy birthday!" she called to him as he continued getting dressed.

Once he was finished, he kissed her on the forehead, told her thank you, and left. It didn't take him long to arrive to Fort Miner High School.

"Hello, Alex! Nice car," one young, pretty blonde called to him as he parked his Stingray.

As Alex closed his car door, he replied, "Thanks." It was obvious he was uninterested in her. He started to stroll quickly across campus when he was approached by a couple of his friends from the football team.

"What's up, Alex?" said Cody, one of the team's wide receivers.

"Nothing much. Ready to get this schoolwork done," Alex said proudly.

"You seem to be in a better mood today," said James, who was the team's number-one wide receiver.

"Yeah! I'm feeling a bit better. I had a good talk with my granny yesterday. And a great night with my girl last night," he said, laughing.

The guys gave him some dap and a high five, minorly congratulating him.

"Well, coach says Shawn Mooney is moving to another state next week—" said James.

"Yep! And you get to be the new QB," added Cody, interrupting.

"Yeah, I know. I finally get the opportunity to throw the ball during games. I mean … I know I'm not better than Shawn, but I'm sure as hell going to do my best," Alex said seriously.

"Yeah, your throwing is pretty crappy sometimes," said Cody.

"Come on, Cody! It's like that?" Alex said.

"Just kidding, bro," Cody replied.

The three young football players walked down the hallway together toward their first-period class.

"Oh, I almost forgot! Happy birthday, man," James said, smiling. Cody repeated the words also.

"Thanks, man," Alex said appreciatively.

"You gonna to be at the game tonight?" James asked.

"Yeah, me and Alicia will be there. She's a cheerleader now, so she has to be there anyway," Alex replied.

Soon the bell rang, indicating the students had five minutes before first period would start.

"All right, Alex—we'll see you later," said Cody.

Alex nodded at them, and they all went separate ways.

On this day, Alex was focused in all of his classes. He concentrated on the classwork and completed all of his assignments without getting frustrated. He was enticed and distracted by a couple of girls, but he didn't allow them to keep his attention for long. After school was over, Alicia called his cell phone, and he answered as he exited his last class.

"What's up, babe?" Alex asked.

"Nothing much! My little brother and I are going to the park until the game starts tonight. Will you meet us there?" Alicia said.

"Yeah, which park?" he replied.

"The best park in Detroit!" she said, and he could hear the smile in her voice.

"Say no more. I know which one you mean," he replied. "I have to stop by my house first, and then I'll be right there."

"OK. I love you, Alex. Happy birthday again!" she said quickly.

"Love you too. Thanks," he said before ending the call.

Alex drove home as quickly as he could. He weaved rapidly through traffic, enjoying his Corvette's smooth handling. He arrived to his grandmother's house, parked on the street, and went inside. Granny was apparently sleeping, since she was nowhere in sight when he entered the home.

Alex went upstairs to his room, opened the door, and threw his backpack on the bed. He quickly took off his school clothes and tossed them into the dirty laundry basket, then crossed the room to his closet to grab some fresh clothes. Just as he reached for a hanger, he saw the birthday present his grandmother had left for him and picked it up.

I almost forgot to open you. I wonder what raggedy old clothes Granny has bought me now for this birthday, he thought. Alex ripped off the wrapping paper and tore the box open. There was one piece of clothing inside that he extracted and eyed.

A New England Patriots jersey, Alex thought, as he held the garment up in the air. *This junk looks dirty! And it smells!* Alex was disgusted. He glanced around the room, still standing in front of the closet in his boxers.

"Granny!" shouted Alex loudly. He threw the jersey on the floor near the dirty clothes basket. *What is this—a birthday gift or some kind of sick joke?* he wondered.

Within seconds, his granny came from her room next door. She walked in and asked, "What is it, Alex? What's all the yelling about?"

"Granny, why would you give me a dirty jersey like that for my birthday?" he asked.

"The guy I bought it from said not to wash it," Granny answered.

"But it stinks!" Alex blurted out.

"Well I'm sorry, Alex! The man said you'd love it and not to wash it because it's some missing Super Bowl jersey everyone has been looking for," she said fretfully.

"*What?*" Alex gasped. He ran over, grabbed the jersey off the floor, and held it up. "No way! This can't be it ..." Alex's voice trailed off in astonishment.

"Give it here, Alex, and I'll go wash it for you. I'm sorry you don't like it," Granny said sadly.

"No! *No!* I don't want it washed anymore!" he half-shouted at her.

"You just said it stunk. Now you don't want it washed? Make up your mind," she said.

"It's *perfect* the way it is, Granny. Thank you—thank you so much! This is the best gift in the whole world!" he said, beaming. He ran over and gave his grandmother a big hug and a kiss.

"Well thank you, Alex! I'm so glad it's OK," she said.

"I love it, Granny! But ... how much did this cost?" Alex asked cautiously.

His grandmother took a deep breath. "The guy charged me an arm and a leg. But I bought it anyway because you only have one eighteenth birthday!" she said.

"This jersey has to be worth a fortune," Alex wondered aloud.

"Well, that's about what I paid for it." Granny chuckled. "My great-great-grandfather Paul Revere was a *real* American Patriot," she said.

"Paul Revere—who is that?" Alex asked.

"You don't know who Paul Revere is?" Granny's face reflected her astonishment.

"No, Granny," he replied.

"What are those people teaching you kids in school nowadays? Well, I thought your mom would have at least told you. Go look him up. He was born in 1735 and lived to be eighty-three. That's why I think I'll be gone soon ..." she murmured, drifting off into her own thoughts.

"Granny, don't say that!" Alex said sharply. Even though he acted clueless, Alex knew his grandmother was in poor health and that her years were likely limited.

"Well, it's true, Alex," she said. I'm eighty-one years old. How much longer do you expect me to live?"

"I don't know, Granny! How about ten more years? Make it to ninety-one," he said.

She chuckled at his optimism and coughed two times afterward.

"Alex, I'll be lucky to live two more years. I've been sick for a while," she said.

The phone rang and interrupted their conversation. "Better go grab that," Granny said as she shuffled out of the room.

After she left, Alex gazed lovingly at the number 12 Patriots jersey. Since he was still shirtless, he tugged the smelly jersey right over his head onto his naked torso. Immediately an unusual sensation came over his body. His heart started beating faster for just a moment before returning to normal. *What was that feeling?* he wondered.

Alex's cell phone rang and startled him out of his reverie.

"Hello," he said as he accepted the call.

"Alex, are you coming or what?" Alicia asked, some frustration creeping into her tone.

"Oh, yes, babe! Sorry—I'm leaving home right now," he assured her.

Alex rushed back to his closet and threw a shirt on over his superb, phenomenal jersey, covering it. Then he put on shorts, shoes, and a cap and left the house.

With the way Alex drove, it didn't take him long at all to arrive at the park. Alicia was waiting on a blanket next to the playground with her six-year-old brother, David.

"Finally! It's about time you made it!" Alicia enthused as she beckoned her boyfriend over.

"Sorry, babe," he said sheepishly.

"I'm just kidding," she said, playfully pushing his shoulder. "I'm happy you're here, and look—I wore all pink just for you." Alicia smiled and posed a bit to display her outfit, and Alex couldn't help but appreciate his girlfriend's perfect frame as he took the opportunity to look her up and down.

David, the little brother, plucked a beautifully decorated cake out of a basket as he beamed. "Happy birthday, Alex! We made a cake for you!" the child said enthusiastically.

"Does it feel good to be eighteen?" Alicia asked.

"Yeah, I guess," Alex replied. "I mean, I'm legally old enough to do almost anything now. I'm an adult!"

"Nuh-uh!" David blurted out. "My mama said you have to be twenty-one to buy beer."

Alicia laughed and rumpled the young boy's hair, and Alex replied, "Yeah, your mama's right. Can't buy beer or liquor for three more years."

The boy ran off to play on the nearby jungle gym, leaving Alex and Alicia sitting alone together on the cozy blanket in the grass. They laughed and joked around as they fed each other pieces of fruit Alicia had packed. The grapes, strawberries, and plums from the brown basket were gone within a couple of minutes. After a short visit to the playground, David ran back over to his sister and Alex with a football in his hands.

"Hey, Alex, will you play catch with me?" David asked.

Alex glanced over at Alicia since he didn't want to just desert her. She reassured him with her eyes and nodded her approval.

"Sure, why not, kiddo? I need to practice throwing the ball anyway. I'm going to be the starting quarterback next week," he added, looking over at Alicia.

"Yep! And I'm going to be right there on the sideline cheering for you!" she said enthusiastically.

Alex and David jogged over to the park's grassy field to play catch. The boy tried to throw the football first, but it fell short of Alex's grasp by several feet.

"Sorry, Alex. I'm not good at throwing the football yet," the boy admitted bashfully.

"It's all right, David! I need to get better myself, but practice makes perfect!" Alex smiled and bent to pick the football up off of the ground. When his fingers grazed the surface of the ball, what felt like an electromagnetic wave surged through his entire body, causing him to shiver as he caught full-body chills.

Whoa! Where did that come from? he thought, confused by the weird feeling.

Alex had no idea that the number12 Patriots jersey—the one Tom Brady had worn during Super Bowl 51 in 2017—possessed a powerful and dominant patriotic spirit.

After the unusual feeling subsided, Alex resumed grabbing the football. As he threw it, the ball flew perfectly and precisely toward little David's hands, making it impossible for him *not* to catch it.

"Wow, Alex! You throw great!" David shouted.

Alex looked down at his hands. He knew he'd released the ball flawlessly, and it had felt amazing as he threw it. David aimed the football, and threw it poorly again back to Alex, who was barely able to catch it. After Alex caught the football, he told David to go back further. David moved backward, and Alex threw the ball nearly fifty yards to where little David stood. The kid didn't even have to chase the ball. He put his hands up in the air and the ball landed right in them. Alex's mouth and eyes grew wide as he watched the ball sail right to David. He pulled on the collar of his shirt and looked down at the jersey underneath.

Oh my God! It's the jersey! It has to be the jersey, he thought.

THREE

The New High School Quarterback

D AVID RAN BACK FROM THE LONG PASS TOWARD ALEX, SHOUTING, "Teach me how to throw like that! Teach me to throw like that! Please, Alex? *Pleeeease!*"

Alex really didn't know what to do—or say. He didn't know how to explain that he didn't have any idea how to teach someone to throw like that. He hadn't even taught himself! He didn't fully understand how he'd been able to throw so accurately either.

"You know what, I have an idea," Alex said. "Put on my lucky jersey, and let's see if it helps you." Alex wanted to see if the Brady jersey might actually be magical. He took off both of his shirts, and handed the garment over to the little boy.

"This jersey stinks!" David shouted, wrinkling his nose.

Alex laughed. "Just put it on. Then go throw the ball for me one time."

David ran approximately fifteen yards away. He aimed the football carefully and then threw a perfect pass to Alex.

Alex caught the ball precisely in the center of his chest. He smiled and nodded. He thought triumphantly, *It is the jersey!*

The boy came running back over, shouting. "I did it! I did it!" He hugged Alex around the waist and said, "Thank you, Alex!"

Alicia walked over, clapping her hands. "Good throw, David!" she called out. She rumpled his unruly hair affectionately again.

"Come on, Alicia! You're messing up my hair," he said.

"Just a lucky throw," said Alex, trying to be secretive.

"No, Alex! This jersey has magic from God on it," David insisted.

Alicia laughed. "Give Alex his stupid jersey back so we can go."

"The jersey is *not* stupid, Alicia! I felt it myself," the boy said.

"No clothes have magic from God on them, David." Her voice was more serious now.

Alex intervened and spoke up. "I think she's right, David. You just had a lucky throw," he said.

The little boy's face fell. "OK, Alex," he said sadly. "Here's your jersey back."

Alicia leaned into Alex and kissed him goodbye softly.

"All, right baby. I'll see you later," said Alex.

"At the football game tonight, right?" she replied.

"Yeah, at the game. I'll be there."

The couple kissed again, and Alicia grabbed her brother's hand to walk away. The boy kept looking back at Alex. David knew the jersey was unique and magnificent. He also knew that Alex was aware of it.

Alex still had the football in his right hand. He put the Patriots jersey on and stuffed his extra shirt into the waistline of his pants. Alex glanced around the park and saw a man nearly eighty yards away. "Hey, man!" Alex shouted. The man looked over. "Catch!" Alex shouted again. He pulled back and slung the football through the air. It released perfectly and floated through the air miraculously. The man only took one step backward. He put both hands up in front of his chin, and the ball landed right in his hands.

"Nice arm!" the man shouted, his eyebrows raised in surprise.

Alex smiled. "Don't mention it," he replied.

Alex walked back to his car and drove home. He took a quick shower and put on clean clothes. By the time he looked at his watch it was already 7:19 p.m., and the football game was scheduled to start at 7:30. He'd have to hurry if he wanted to get there on time. On his way to the stadium, however, his Corvette had a flat rear tire, which he had to change. Luckily, his spare was an absolute duplicate of the other tires, so the car didn't look unusual. Alex arrived to the game far later than he'd hoped to, and it was already halftime. The score was 17 to 6, and the Fort Miner Flamethrowers were losing.

Alex didn't bother talking to anyone. He entered the stadium and rushed to the sidelines next to his coach. Alicia waved to him and continued her cheerleading duties. He admired her flawless skin and lovely body. He loved watching her cheer during games in her red-and-yellow uniform.

Before the game resumed, she came and spoke to him. "Hey, Alex! Glad you could make it. What took so long?" she asked, out of breath.

"Flat tire," he replied.

"Gimme a kiss," she said with a slight pout.

Alex leaned forward, placed one hand underneath her chin, and kissed her sweetly.

"I see my Flamethrowers are losing," he said as he released Alicia's chin.

"Yeah, we only scored two field goals. James is doing a great job running the ball, but Cody is dropping passes like crazy!" she explained.

"How's Shawn throwing the ball tonight?" Alex asked curiously.

"He's doing good. Jose has dropped two touchdown passes. We really should be winning 20 to 17," she replied.

Within a few minutes, the game had resumed.

"Alicia! Come on, girl!" the head cheerleader called out.

"All right, Alex, gotta go," she said and scampered back to the cheerleading squad.

The Flamethrowers received the ball after the half. James Jones caught the kickoff and began running it down field. He stiff-armed one defender and spun around another before running headfirst into another opponent. He was brought down at the fifty yard line. The cheerleaders broke out into a celebration on behalf of his great run to the halfway point of the field.

The team positioned themselves for an offensive play. Shawn Mooney, the quarterback, dropped back and passed to Cody Harris. Unfortunately the pass was too high, and Cody couldn't catch it. On the next down they repeated the same play, except that Shawn threw the ball eighteen yards to Jose Hernandez. Jose caught the ball and ran for ten more yards on top of the pass.

The Flamethrowers were now at the twenty-two yard line. They were getting closer to the goal. The team did a running play next. Shawn handed the ball off to James Jones, who picked up three yards before getting tackled. The team repeated the play again. James rushed forward again, gaining four more yards for the team. It was third down and three yards to go. The team was at the fifteen yard line. They decided to run the ball again. James only picked up two more yards, making it fourth and one.

"Kick a field goal," said the coach.

"No, Coach Parker! Let me run it again. I'll get the first down," James said.

The coach hesitated before relenting. "All right, James! I'm going against my better judgment, but go ahead."

James did it! He ran for two more yards and got the first down. Everyone clapped and cheered.

During a quick huddle, Shawn spoke dominantly. "Cody! The ball is going to you this play. You've dropped two touchdown passes tonight. Catch the damn ball, bro!"

"All right, man! I got you," Cody said, putting on his game face.

Alex was on the sideline watching, rooting for his team to score. Cody looked over and saw Alex, who was throwing the Flamethrower's hand signal up in the air. Cody and James smiled, as they'd created the hand sign themselves.

"Down, set, *hike!*" Shawn barked.

The center tossed the ball backward through his legs to the quarterback. Shawn stepped back quickly as a big, fast defensive tackle broke through the offensive line. Shawn was forced to scramble like eggs. He ran around to the left side, and before he crossed the line of scrimmage, he spotted Cody in the end zone. Shawn stopped running and slung the ball as hard as he could toward Cody, who caught the precise pass easily.

"Touchdown, Flamethrowers!" shouted the announcers as the referees threw up their arms in confirmation. Every Flamethrower fan began celebrating. For some reason the touchdown only seemed to piss off the opponents. However, the Flamethrowers didn't score any more touchdowns or field goals that night, and they ended up losing 38 to 13.

Alex, Alicia, and David went to eat at a fancy restaurant after the game. They sat at a nice table and conversed about the game.

"We've lost three in a row," Alex said, dejectedly.

Alicia pointed at Alex with her fork in hand. "Well, you start quarterbacking for the team next week. Maybe you should win some games and do something about it!" she said flippantly.

"Trust me—I'm going to try. Our high school has never even been to the state championship before," Alex said.

Little David spoke up. "If you wear that jersey every game, I know you'll throw good!"

"Hush, David! Grown-ups are talking. Besides, there's no such thing as a magical jersey," Alicia said firmly.

David kept quiet and continued eating his food. After dinner, the couple hugged and kissed before going their separate ways.

Since Alicia's parents were scheduled to return in the morning, the couple didn't want to take the chance of getting caught by having another sleepover. Alex went straight home and arrived around ten thirty. His granny was fast asleep when he peeked into her room to check up on her. He stared blankly for a moment as Granny's words from their prior conversation floated through his mind. *Alex, I'll be lucky to live two more years. I've been sick for a long time.*

Alex closed the door and headed back to his own room.

★★★

Friday, September 23, 2017 (One week later)

Coach Parker walked into the locker room to address his team before the game began. Alex, Cody, James, and all of the other players were fully dressed in their red-and-yellow uniforms and had their helmets in their hands.

"Flamethrowers, listen up!" Coach Parker shouted. All of the young players gave the coach their undivided attention. "This is our fourth game tonight. We are *zero* and three. We may not go to the playoffs, but we need to at least get a win for our fans and our families who are here watching tonight. Kids, we have a great team, and I believe in all of you. Go out there, and play your best. All right?" Coach shouted.

"Yeah!" the team shouted back.

"On the count of three, everybody yell *Flamethrowers*. One! Two! Three—"

"Flamethrowers!" everyone shouted in unison.

Within seconds the teams were running onto the football field. The opposing team received the ball first at the beginning of the game. Their opponents were called the Pandas, and they were good football players. The team didn't run the ball at all during their first drive. Their passing and catching games were excellent. The first pass was an eighteen yard completion, followed by a twenty-seven yard completion. The third pass was incomplete. The fourth pass was hauled in at nineteen yards. On the fifth pass, their quarterback threw a twelve yard pass into the end zone, where it was caught by a wide receiver.

"Touchdown, Pandas!" the announcer called out over the loud speaker.

As the Pandas prepared to kick their field goal, Alex was getting ready to start. He looked in his bag and realized his special jersey was missing. "The jersey!" Alex cried out. "Dang it! Aw, man, I left it!"

He grabbed his phone from his bag on the sideline and called his granny's home number.

"Pick up, Granny! Pick up, Granny!" he whispered as the phone rang. It took her a long time, but she did answer at last.

"Hello. May I ask who's calling?" she said.

"Granny, it's Alex!" he said quickly. "Will you please look on the sofa in the living room and see if I left my football backpack in there?"

"I see it, Alex. Do you need it, son?" she said after a moment's silence on the other end.

"Yes, ma'am. I think I left my jersey in it," he replied.

"Hold up! Let me go take a look." There was a soft thud as he heard her set the receiver down to go inspect his bag more closely. "Only jersey I see is the stinky one I bought for your birthday. Is that the one you're looking for?" she asked when she returned.

"Yes, ma'am!" Alex said urgently. "Could you please bring it to the football game? I need it. It's an emergency!"

"OK, Alex. I'll be there as soon as I can."

"All right, Granny. See you when you get here," he said as he snapped the phone shut.

"Come on, Alex! It's your turn to show us what you've got!" Coach Parker shouted.

Alex hesitated. He didn't want to start the game without having the jersey; however, he didn't have a choice. He pulled his helmet on and trotted out to the field.

He didn't throw well at all during any of the drives. The team couldn't get the ball past the fifty yard line and had to punt over and over.

C'mon, Granny. Where are you? Alex silently willed his grandmother to appear.

"And the halftime score is twenty-four to zero!" The announcer's voice echoed around the stadium.

The Flamethrowers walked off the field toward their locker room with their heads down and shoulders slumped. Alex glanced over at Alicia and the other cheerleaders but kept walking. He was too embarrassed to speak to anyone.

The head cheerleader looked sharply at Alicia. "Your boyfriend sucks at quarterback! He should be the waterboy!" she jeered.

"Watch your mouth about him, Christina!" Alicia snapped back fiercely. "Before you're not able to *drink* any water."

The team was completely silent as the players took their break in the locker room. Nobody had anything to say. Some of the players openly shook their heads at Alex.

"Alex, you have to tighten up, man. You've only completed four out of sixteen passes!" Cody whispered urgently.

"I will, man. I will," Alex muttered back.

Halftime flew by, and it was time for the game to resume. The players ran back on to the field and assumed kickoff position. The Pandas kicked the ball off to the Flamethrowers. James Jones caught the ball at the twenty and took off, running full-speed. He didn't make it very far and was quickly tackled at the twenty-five yard line. Now it was time for the Flamethrowers offense to get on the field.

Alex stared into the crowd, desperately searching for his grandmother. *Granny, where are you?* he thought. Alex already felt defeated as he placed his helmet on and ran to the field.

"Down, set, *hike!*" Alex yelled. He stepped back and examined the field. He saw Jose Hernandez waving for the ball and threw it to him. The ball was almost intercepted by a defensive Panda.

"*Ohhhh!*" The crowd moaned in unison.

"Take the quarterback out of the game!" yelled an old man from the stand.

"Yeah! Number fifteen can't throw!" shouted someone else.

Alex looked hopelessly at the increasingly angry crowd when he suddenly saw his grandmother appear through the throng.

"Hey, watch your tongue!" Granny admonished the hecklers harshly. "That's my grandson you're talking about."

Alex grinned and called a time-out.

"And the Flamethrowers are calling a time-out! The score is still twenty-four to zero," the announcer called out.

Alex ran to the sideline where his grandmother was coming down.

"Hey, Granny! What took so long?" he asked, concerned but urgent.

"I had a minor asthma attack, but I'm all right, baby. Here's your backpack," she said, wheezing a bit.

Alex grabbed the backpack, peeked in, and saw his amazing number 12 Patriots jersey. He gave his grandmother a quick hug. "Thank you so much, Granny!" he called out as he rushed back toward the field.

Alex looked at his coach and shouted, "Hold on, Coach! My contact lens popped out on the field, and I need to replace it."

"All right, Alex, make it quick!" Coach Parker called back as Alex ran off of the field into the locker-room.

"We don't need fifteen to play! Play without a quarterback!" shouted an onlooker.

Once inside of the bathroom, Alex pulled out the number 12 New England Patriots jersey. He smiled and said a quick, silent prayer. *Please, God! If this is the same missing jersey Tom Brady wore in Super Bowl fifty-one when he made history, please bless this jersey. May it help me throw the ball like the best quarterback of all time.* He put the Patriots jersey on under his own before quickly running back toward the field.

"Took you long enough," the coach said sternly.

"Sorry, Coach!" Alex shouted. He placed his helmet on his head and headed back to the game.

"Down, set, *hike!*" he shouted. Alex grabbed the ball from the center and stepped back two feet. He spotted Cody Harris barely open and slung the ball at the wide receiver. The football went flying past a Panda defender's fingers and hit Cody right in the chest. The crowd cheered, celebrating the twenty-yard catch. The Flamethrowers were now at the forty-five yard line. Alex hurried the offense back to the line without a huddle.

"Down, set, *hike!*" Alex shouted again. This time, he dropped back and spotted Jose Hernandez slanting through the center of the field. Alex didn't hesitate to sling the ball right in front of Jose's face mask. Jose caught the perfectly thrown ball and took off running full-speed. He managed to jet past the safety and ran into the end zone for a touchdown.

The home fans erupted in cheers and gave the team a round of applause. The score was now 24–7. The Flamethrowers' defense knew they had to step up and stop the Pandas from scoring, and that is what they did. They stopped the offense, forcing them to punt after three hard downs. Alex knew this was their opportunity, and he began throwing the football like he never had before. The crowd was amazed by the magnificent transmogrification Alex had made.

The hidden jersey underneath his shoulder pads was giving him a sensational tingling feeling every time he touched the football. The number 12 jersey was truly divine and one of a kind. The Flamethrowers scored two touchdowns in the third quarter and two more in the fourth. The final score was 28–24. The Fort Miner Flamethrowers had won game number four. It was their first win of the season. The players celebrated on the field, pouring Gatorade on each other. They were excited and ready to play the next game.

The Flamethrowers won their next away game with a score of 42–14. They defeated their opponent easily, as Alex had thrown the ball like a professional quarterback. Their third game was a blowout. The final score was 35–0, and the team went on to win their fifth, sixth, and seventh games as well. In every single winning game, Alex had on the number 12 Patriots, and he was throwing the ball magnificently. The Flamethrowers didn't lose any more games for the rest of the season with Alex Revere as their quarterback. They conquered the toughest teams in the state of Michigan and went to the high school state championship game.

The day of the big championship game came around quickly. The Flamethrowers knew this game would be incredibly tough. The Cobras were their opponents and they were a highly competitive team with an awesome defense.

In the first quarter the Cobras kept the Flamethrowers' wide receivers from getting open for Alex's passes. Alex was under a lot of pressure from the defensive line and was afraid of throwing an interception. He was scrambling more than he usually did as a six four quarterback, and though he was quick, he couldn't always get the first down. The halftime score was 28–13 in favor of the Cobras.

At halftime, Coach Parker was fired up and questioned Alex. "You've got to throw the ball more! Why aren't you throwing the ball?"

"Because, Coach, our receivers aren't all the way open, and I'm afraid I'll throw interceptions," Alex replied.

"Listen, Alex! We're down by fifteen points. No Fort Miner High School football team has *ever* made it this far. You've *already* made history for this school, kid, but we didn't come this far to lose. Get in there, and *throw that damn ball*! I don't care about about an interception, and I don't want you to either!" Coach Parker barked.

"OK, Coach! I'll do just that," Alex said. He smiled and took a sip of Gatorade. He was ready for the second half.

FOUR

Graduating and Choosing the Best College

THE COBRAS RECEIVED THE BALL FIRST AFTER HALFTIME AND SCORED a touchdown on their first drive, taking the score to 35–13. Alex was worried, as was everyone else on the team. He went on to the field and began throwing the football like he'd told his coach he would. The number 12 Patriots jersey that was underneath his own school uniform took effect every time he threw the ball.

Each of the first two passes he threw resulted in ten-yard gains, first downs. The third one he released, however, was a sixty-nine-yard touchdown pass to Jose Hernandez, who caught the ball and dashed into the end zone. The crowd went wild as the score changed to 35–19. Alex went and spoke to the defensive players while the kicker kicked the extra point.

"You guys have to stop them from scoring! If you all won't let them score more points, I promise you we'll win this game!" Alex shouted to them confidence.

The defense believed in their quarterback. Alex had proven to them he was a great passer. When the defense went on the field, they shut down their opponents' offense and forced them to punt, as they'd do for the rest of the game.

Alex threw two more touchdowns, making the score 35–33. With one minute left on the clock, Alex slung the ball downfield to Cody for a forty-one-yard completion. Cody was tackled at the thirty-two yard line. With thirty-eight seconds left on the clock, Alex knelt the ball, stopping the clock.

"What are you doing?" asked the coach.

"I don't need that much time. The next play will be a touchdown," he replied.

"And how in the hell do you know that?" Coach Parker wondered aloud, sounding worried. Alex winked and ran back on the field.

With eighteen seconds left on the clock, the center hiked the ball to Alex. A rusher broke through the offensive line unexpectedly, forcing Alex to throw the ball away. With now just fourteen seconds left, Alex repeated the previous play. Before the ball was hiked, he pointed to his offensive lineman to ask for protection from another blitz. The lineman shifted as Alex had told him to do.

Then Alex shouted, "Down, set, *hike!*"

He stepped back quickly once he had the ball. He saw Jose open but knew the safety would expect him to go that way. Although Cody was covered, he was very close to the end zone. Alex saw an opportunity and slung the ball with nine seconds left on the clock. A defensive player for the Cobras grabbed at Cody's jersey, trying to interfere with the catch.

Cody pushed the player's hands off and dove for the ball, his whole body and hands stretched out as far as he could. He caught the ball in the end zone.

"Touchdown, Flamethrowers!" the announcer called out over the intercom.

Coach Parker, the players, the principal, their families, fans, and cheerleaders all went crazy celebrating. Hands were up. Hugging, screaming and shouting was going on everywhere. The players of the team lifted Cody and Alex up in the air and carried them off of the field. Then they put them down near the coach.

"Congratulations, kids! You won the state championship!" Coach Parker shouted, smiling from ear to ear. He looked at Alex and said, "I'm proud of you kid. After you graduate in May, there will never be another number 15 who plays for our high school's football team ever again. I can promise you that."

"Thanks, Coach," Alex replied.

"A lot of colleges are going to be trying to get you to come to their school. Do you have any in mind?" Coach Parker asked.

"No, not really. I think I'm going to stay here at home and go to Michigan State. My grandma's not doing too well," Alex said.

"That would be lovely! If so, I will most certainly be at every single home game," the coach said.

After the conversation with the coach, Alex saw Alicia approaching. They hugged, kissed, and talked about the game. After the compliments about the accomplishments, Alicia told him that his granny was in the hospital.

"What! Who told you this?" Alex asked, shocked and worried.

"I got a text," Alicia said.

"Stay here! Let me get my things so we can leave right now," he replied.

Alex took off running toward the locker room to grab his belongings. He returned within a minute.

"Let's go!" Alex shouted, ready to move fast.

The two of them hurried back to Alex's Corvette. While driving over the speed limit, Alex was pulled over by a cop and received a speeding ticket on the way to the hospital. When they arrived, Alex and Alicia rushed inside to ask after Granny with great concern. It took a moment for a doctor to call his name, but when one did, the couple rushed over to speak with him.

The doctor introduced himself as Dr. Polk and told them what had been going on with Granny's health conditions. "Listen, young man, your grandmother isn't doing very well. She isn't breathing on her own. Her lungs are congested. It may take a couple days to clear the clogs and blockages that are preventing her from breathing." Dr. Polk paused for a second and looked seriously into Alex's eyes. "Listen to me, Alex. You have to take care of your grandmother and help her with her breathing treatment on a daily basis. She has lung cancer. There's no telling how much longer she's going to be around."

Alex's eyes began to water as he listened to the stark words from the elderly doctor. Alex nodded his head, indicating that he'd understood and asked, "Sir, if it's all right, can I go see her?"

"Sure, son. Go right ahead," the doctor replied.

Alex and Alicia walked down the long hospital hallway toward Granny's temporary bedroom. When they walked in, she was resting. Alex walked over to the side of the bed and gazed into her familiar, wrinkled face. Her green eyes struggled to open as she felt a presence near her. Her voice crackled harshly with age as she spoke. "Hey there, Alex," she said.

Alex smiled. "Hey, Granny. Are you OK? How do you feel?" he asked.

"Oh, Alex, I'm fine, son. Just my lungs are old and ready to give up on me," she said, and Alex lowered his head and looked at the ground sadly.

"Oh, Alex, don't put your head down, grandson," Granny continued. "Keep it up. It's not the end of the world. Your life is just beginning. We live to die, baby. Just enjoy your health and youth like I did so that when your time comes, it won't even bother you."

Hot tears fell from Alex's eyes as he blinked heavily. "Yes, ma'am," he replied softly.

"It's a miracle I didn't die today. My lungs gave up on me, and I couldn't breathe on my own. Either I'm one lucky old woman, or it was magical like that Patriots jersey I bought you for your birthday," she said with a chuckle.

Alex's eyes opened wide, shocked by his granny's words. "You know about the jersey being magical?"

"Of course I do, Alex! That's why I paid exactly $715,419 for it," she said, coughing.

"You paid that much for the jersey?" Alex was astonished.

"Yes, I did. I watched Super Bowl fifty-one. My great-great-grandfather Paul Revere and many other dead American patriots were at that game, Alex. I saw spirits and angels standing on the field during the third and fourth quarters. That's how I knew Tim Bradley and that jersey was blessed from God," she said.

"His name isn't Tim Bradley, Granny." Alex laughed. Alicia laughed also, and Granny noticed her for the first time.

"Oh, Alicia, I didn't even notice you standing over there," Granny said to Alicia, who waved. "I reckon my eyes are getting bad also," the older lady added.

They continued talking for a little while longer, then said their farewells. Since Granny's doctor wanted her to remain at the hospital. Alex hugged and kissed her and then departed, waving to her as they walked out.

Alex and Alicia went to sleep at Granny's house that night. Alicia called her parents and informed them of where she'd be.

★Six Months Later★

The next six months of Alex's senior year zoomed. December, January, February, March, April, and May seemed to only take a few minutes each. Before Alex knew what was happening, it was his graduation day.

★May 2018★

"Alex Revere!" The lady at the podium onstage called out his name.

Alex stood and walked across the stage toward the podium in his red cap and gown. He was smiling uncontrollably as he looked into the crowd. He saw Granny sitting with Alicia, David, and their parents. Alex rubbed his eyes as he thought he saw his deceased mom and dad in angelic spiritual form. When he did a double take and looked again they were gone, or perhaps they were never really there at all.

Alex said, "Thank you," as he received his diploma. He gave a short speech dedicated to his family, God, and others who encouraged him and helped him graduate with a 3.8 GPA. The coach, his fans, his family, and people from many different colleges were present, and many took pictures of Alex.

After the graduation, Alex had a meeting with his personal representative. There were also three representatives from different colleges present, along with Alex's family. There were recruiters from the University of Michigan, the University of Texas, and Penn State.

"Listen, Alex. I know you wanted to be a starting quarterback at Michigan State, but unfortunately, you wouldn't be starting for a year or two," his representative told him.

"What?" Alex was shocked.

"Yes, Mr. Revere. We have a great quarterback already who has two more years of college. But he might leave a year early. After he's gone, we'd love to have you next in line," said the Michigan State recruiter said.

"No, sir. I can't do that. I deserve to start," Alex said.

"Well, Alex, you still have both of these gentlemen here offering you a starting position at their college. The two recruiters from Pennsylvania and Texas looked at Alex and smiled. "Choose one of those three hats on the table, son. Or should I say two hats?" Alex's representative said.

Alex glanced back at his family.

"Go ahead, Alex. Do what's best for you," Granny said with a smile.

Alex contemplated and reminisced. He suddenly heard his granny's voice in his head saying, *He was born in 1735 and died at age eighty-three. That's why I think I'll be gone soon.* He continued thinking and remembering other conversations with his granny. *I'm eighty-one years old. How much longer do you expect me to live?* And *I'll be lucky to live two more years.*

Tears formed in Alex's eyes. He reached to the table and grabbed the Michigan State cap. Everyone was shocked but began clapping and celebrating.

"Oh my God! He's still going to stay!" Alicia said happily.

Alex stared deeply into his granny's aged green eyes and smiled. She silently nodded her head at him, letting him know she understood why he'd chosen Michigan State. Everyone could see the tears in Alex's eyes; however, only Granny sincerely knew the reason he was crying. The recruiters from Penn State and Texas left, upset and disappointed.

In August of 2018, Alex began attending Michigan State University in East Lansing, Michigan. Since Alex was a Michigan resident, his fees were less than those for out-of-state students. Without his scholarship, he would've had to pay approximately $38,000 annually with room and board. After contemplating and negotiating with his financial advisor, he decided to live on campus.

The college had over fifty thousand students enrolled, and Alex was surprised to see that Cody Harris had decided to choose the same college near home, just like him. The only difference was that Cody would be a starting wide receiver, and Alex wouldn't be the starting quarterback.

The two young adults stuck together and were always around one another like brothers. Both had met beautiful new girlfriends at college. Alex felt bad about cheating on Alicia, but he couldn't help but become interested in other young women with all the pretty college girls around him who were very flirtatious, enticing, and generous. They would help the boys with homework, so they didn't even have to do their own assignments.

It didn't take long for the football season to roll around, and Michigan State started football practice. Alex and Cody met up at the college field before their first practice.

"Alex, you did so great at quarterback. You should be the starting QB," Cody said.

"I know, Cody. But the quarterback we have now has been the quarterback for two years already. And he's pretty good," Alex said truthfully.

"Is he better than you?" asked Cody.

Alex laughed at the comment. "No way! Not at all."

As Alex threw the ball to different players on the team everyone was amazed by his incredible arm and throwing ability. Alex had put the number 12 New England Patriots jersey on underneath his practice gear. He wanted to make sure he demonstrated his skills.

"Wow, that kid can throw a football," said Coach Singer, the coach of the college team.

The first game of the season was a home game at Michigan State. Alex had to sit on the bench and watch the starting quarterback perform. He watched as he made great passes and shared the ball. Alex actually admired the quarterback for his coordination, awareness, and good sportsmanship.

It was obvious the players, fans, coaches, and cheerleaders loved the guy. The team held the lead the entire game. Their opponents couldn't outscore them. Michigan State was winning the game at the beginning of the fourth quarter. The score was 21–17, and it was third down with five yards to go. Michigan State had the ball on their own thirty-two yard line—not in field goal range. The quarterback yelled, *"Hike!"* Immediately a defensive tackle rushed through the offensive line and sacked the Michigan State quarterback. The tackle then stood up and flexed his muscles, showing he was a tough tackler.

A couple different people, including two physical therapists, ran onto the field when the quarterback didn't get up off of the ground.

"Uh oh! I think the quarterback from Michigan State is injured," called Bob, one of the announcers, over the loud speaker.

"Yeah, Bob. Looks to me like it's his ribs," Ron, the other announcer, replied.

"These are the kind of injuries I hate to see," Bob said. "These are the kinds of injuries that can knock players out for weeks at a time."

The quarterback was carried off the field on a stretcher. Coach Singer walked over to Alex and spoke. "Alex Revere! I'm going to need you to go in and play for Tony!"

"All right, Coach," Alex replied, smiling a little.

Michigan State punted the ball to the other team because it was fourth and twelve.

While the defense ran on the field to play, Alex ran back to the locker room. He rushed to his locker and began turning the master combination lock. Once he opened the locker, he dug through it, tossing clothes aside. After a few seconds, he found the number 12 New England Patriots jersey he was looking for.

Alex smiled and embraced the number 12 jersey, hugging it to his chest. Alex took off his football gear, and put the magical jersey on. Afterward, Alex placed his gear back on top and put on his number 15 Michigan State jersey over it.

He smiled, ready to go play. *This game is on TV today. I know Granny's watching it*, Alex thought. He ran out of the locker room back toward the football field.

As he returned to the sideline, the away team scored a touchdown. Fans of the away team began clapping and celebrating loudly. Michigan State was now losing, 24–21 after the extra point. The away team kicked the ball through the air to the receiver from Michigan State. He sprinted off for a twenty-seven yard run before being tackled.

"All right, offense. Get in there and show'em who's boss in Lansing!" Coach Singer shouted.

Cody looked at Alex and smiled. "Here's your chance right here!" Cody whispered.

"This is what I've been waiting for," said Alex, smiling. He put his helmet on and ran to the field behind the rest of the offensive players.

"*Hike!*" Alex shouted. He grabbed the ball from the center and stepped back into his throwing position. He spotted Shane Bowen and threw the ball twenty-three yards to him.

The ball almost hit him in the face mask, but he caught it. Before he could run further, though, he was tackled. Michigan State moved forward to the fifty yard line. Without a huddle, Alex hurried the offensive line together and had the ball hiked. He dropped back into the pocket and threw the ball forty-two yards to his old friend Cody. Cody had to dive to catch the ball, but he managed to accomplish it. The safety touched him before he could get back up.

Michigan State fans were getting excited in the stands. The team was now just eight yards from the end zone. It was now first and goal. As soon as Alex screamed "*Hike!*" a defensive player rushed Alex and forced him to throw the ball away.

On second down a defensive player rushed again and sacked Alex, causing a three-yard loss. Alex was frustrated that he wasn't getting enough time to throw the ball.

The team did a quick huddle, clapped their hands, and lined back up. It was third and goal, and they were eleven yards from the end zone.

A defensive player broke through the offensive line and rushed Alex from the right.

Alex scrambled left and took off running as fast as he could, the football in one hand. Just as a defensive player leapt at him, he slid into the end zone. The announcer shouted loudly over the stadium speakers. *"Touchdown! Michigan State!"*

The score was now 27–24, as Michigan State's extra point attempt had been blocked. There were four minutes left in the game, and Michigan State was back on top.

Then the away team scored another touchdown again in less than three minutes. The score was 31–24, and Michigan State was now losing again.

Alex had fifty-nine seconds to score a touchdown. When he got the ball in his hands, he began throwing like never before, completing pass after pass. Alex was moving the ball, and the team moved downfield like a marching band. At second and goal he handed the ball off to Jamar Thomas, a running back.

The strong legged running back carried the ball in for the touchdown making, and the score was now 31–30.

"All right, get the kicker in there, and tie this game up!" Coach shouted.

"Coach, let me go for the two point conversion," Alex said with confidence.

"What, Revere? No, kid. It's not a guarantee. The field goal is safer," Coach replied.

"And what if it's blocked again?" asked Alex.

The coach thought about it. "All right, Alex! You've done an excellent job of keeping us in the game. This is your call. But if you mess this up, you're in big trouble!" he warned.

"I'm AR-15! I can't mess this up," said Alex boldly.

Without further elaboration, Alex ran onto the field. "The kid sure has a lot of guts," said the defensive coordinator.

"I see that now," said the coach.

The announcer began shouting over the stadium speakers. "And Michigan State doesn't seem to be kicking the field goal! I think they're going for the win, Bob!" shouted Ron over the loud speaker.

"Yep! They're not settling for a tie game and overtime," Bob replied.

Right after that, Alex hiked the ball. He didn't hesitate. Cody did a quick slant through the middle of the end zone. Alex spotted him and quickly slung the ball right to him. Cody caught the ball easily, and instantly the fans went wild.

"And it's good!" the announcers shouted.

The coach for the away team slammed his cap on the ground in disappointment. There were four seconds left on the clock. It was over. Michigan State had won the game 32–31.

That night there was a party to celebrate the university's first win of the season. Alex and Cody went to the celebration to hang out and have a good time. While there, one of the prettiest blondes Alex had ever seen approached him. The five seven model resembled a genuine Barbie. She had on a short pink dress, pink lipstick, and pink nail polish.

"Hey there Alex, Revere," she said, batting her eyes at him.

"Hey, beautiful! What's your name?" he asked.

"Alexus," she replied. Alex coughed after she said her name.

"Are you all right?" she asked.

"Yeah, I'm fine. *Alexus* just sounds a lot like *Alicia*," he said.

"Why, do you have a girlfriend here?" she asked.

"No! I'm a freshman. I just started college," he said.

Cody stood next to Alex and listened to their entire exchange.

"Oh, well, Alex, I'm a senior. I've been attending Michigan State for four years, and I've never seen a quarterback throw like you," she said.

"Oh yeah. You like the way I throw the ball?" he asked, really asking.

"Actually I do! And I like you too," she said boldly. Alex began to blush. He had never met girls so bad before he arrived at college.

Since he hesitated to respond, she spoke again. "Well, here's my number! Just give me a call when you get a chance." She handed him a small piece of paper.

Alex accepted the note and said, "OK then. I will."

As she walked away, she stopped and looked at him. "And you better not forget my name. Alex and us. Put it together—*Alexus*," she said, smiling. Alex smiled at the coincidence. After she walked away, Shane Bowen walked over. The tall wide receiver was also a senior.

"What's up, Shane?" asked Alex.

"What's up, kid? Good game, man!" replied Shane respectfully.

"Thanks! As long as I'm quarterback, we're going to win like that every single game!" said Alex.

"I hope so. I'd love to play in a bowl game before I graduate. Oh yeah, and I've got to tell you—that girl you were just talking to is bad news. I've known her since we started college together four years ago," Shane said, his tone serious.

"Why do you say that? Does she have an STD?" Alex asked.

Shane laughed at the comment. "No, not that I know of. But she's the starting quarterback's girlfriend, Alex. And she's bad news, bro. Trust me," said the senior.

"Well, Alex already has a wifey. Alexus will be a one nighty," Cody joked, laughing.

Alex smiled at the joke. "All right, bro. I'll chat with y'all later. Enjoy the party," said Shane. They shook hands and went separate ways.

"Forget what Shane is talking about. He's just mad he can't get her," Cody said.

"Yeah, I know. Either that, or that quarterback is his buddy," Alex replied.

The next week came very fast, and it was time for their second game. Alex made sure he placed his number 12 Patriots jersey on underneath his number 15 Michigan State jersey. When Alex played game two, he demolished the other college football team. With three minutes left in the fourth quarter the score was 49–6.

"Coach, let the third-string quarterback get some action. I've picked these guys apart already," Alex said.

The coach nodded. "You sure have! This game is already won."

He looked at the third string quarterback on the bench. "Victor Smith! Get in their kid," said the coach. Victor was happy to get in the game and quarterback.

The announcer began shouting over the field. "Looks like Michigan State is taking their lethal weapon, AR-15, out of the game!" the commentator shouted.

"Yeah, George, the game is definitely won. Alex Revere has thrown seven touchdown passes tonight," said the other announcer.

"Yes, Bill, he has. That Alex Revere kid is incredible. I think Michigan State may just have the right quarterback to make it to a bowl game," George said.

"I like Revere, but it's way too early to speak of bowl games right now," Bill replied.

The opponents scored one more field goal, making the final score 49–9. Michigan State now had two wins and zero losses for their starting record. After the game, Alex was approached by the beautiful senior Alexus again.

"Hey there, Alex," she said.

"What's up, Alexus?" he replied.

She gave him a hug and kiss. It was obvious they had been communicating and hanging out together. "Nothing much! Are you coming over to my place tonight?" she asked.

"I mean, why not? There's probably nothing better to do than to chill with you.," said Alex with a grin.

She smiled back. "Great! I'll have everything ready before you come. What time do you think you'll be there?" she asked.

"It'll be after ten. I'm going to see my grandmother," he replied.

"All right then. I'll be up waiting."

They hugged and kissed each other again. Several other football players were watching and began shaking their heads.

"She's nothing but a gold digger. She sees three letters—*NFL*—and millions of dollars written all over him," Shane Bowen said.

"Maybe so, Shane. But he just can't leave her alone," replied Cody.

"Yeah, I bet he can't. Because the day he does break up with her, it's going to be a problem," replied Shane.

Those were the last words of that conversation. Cody didn't ask Shane what he meant or anything. Shortly thereafter they gathered their things and left the school's football area. Alex got inside his Corvette and headed toward his granny's house. He used his spare key and entered the home and saw his only uncle, Alvin, sitting on the sofa.

"Hey there, Alex," said Uncle Alvin. "What's up?"

"Nothing much. I haven't seen you in a while. Where's Granny?" Alex asked.

"She's in the bathroom. I got evicted from my apartment. Since Mom isn't doing well, I decided to move in and help her around the house," Alvin said.

Alex nodded and walked away. He saw Granny coming out of the bathroom as he walked in that direction and caught her eye.

"Alex! Hello, baby! I'm glad to see you!" she said, smiling.

Alex reached out and gave her a hug. "Love you, Granny," he said.

"Oh, baby, I love you too, sweetheart. I saw you on TV today. You played great!" she exclaimed.

"Thanks! What's Alvin doing here? He says he got evicted out of his place."

"I think he's back on those drugs again," she said.

Alex meditated on her words. "Well, let him stay for a while. If you need me, call me. If you find out he's stealing from you, call the police on him, Granny," said Alex.

"I most certainly will—although I'd hate to do it."

"You're too old to be dealing with that mess, Granny," he said.

Alex stuck around Granny's house in Detroit for a while. He went to his old bedroom and packed up all his valuable trophies and sports collector cards. Afterward he said his goodbyes to both of them, told his granny how much he loved her, and left.

Alex thought about Alicia a lot. He missed her tremendously, but him being in college had caused them to grow distant. The two of them still communicated on the phone almost every day, though, as they'd never officially broken up. Honestly, they were still boyfriend and girlfriend. They were just a couple of distant lovers.

Alex didn't call Alicia and let her know he was in the area. Instead he left Detroit and drove back to East Lansing. His next stop was Alexus's place.

When he arrived, Alexus was wearing lingerie. There were candles lit, music was playing, and the mood was perfect. Alexus smelled so good from the strawberry bubble bath she'd taken. Her apartment was clean and flawlessly decorated. The two of them began laughing, cuddling, and doing whatever they pleased that night.

The next Saturday arrived very quickly. Alex defeated his opponents without a problem. Nobody could believe the way Alex was throwing the ball. Every pass was a perfect and complete. It was so amazing how the ball would fly right pass the opponents' faces or arms to be caught by a Michigan State receiver. The final score of game three was 63–20. The front cover of the newspaper read, *Michigan State and AR-15 Have Done It Again.*

Everybody was now talking and whispering about Alex Revere, also known as AR-15. But the wins didn't stop there. Alex kept winning all season. Every college team he played he conquered.

In game four they beat Duke 28–17.

In game five they beat Florida State University 38–21.

In game six they beat Northwestern 54–24.

And so on and so on. The Michigan State team went undefeated for the rest of the season.

"Well, gentlemen! We have to go win that bowl game!" shouted the coach. All the football players in the locker room began cheering loudly.

FIVE

The Bowl Game and the Crooked Deal

➡

DECEMBER TWENTY-FIFTH ROLLED AROUND QUICKLY. ALEX celebrated Christmas with his granny and his uncle Alvin. Alicia and her little brother, David, showed up at Granny's house also. The two high school sweethearts exchanged Christmas gifts and many hugs and kisses.

Alex pulled a ticket out of his pocket and handed it to his eighty-one-year-old grandmother. "Granny, I want you to come to my bowl game. Here, take this ticket," Alex said.

"I want to go to the bowl game too, Alex!" Alicia shouted.

"Chill, Alicia! I have one for you too," he said, smiling. Alex reached in his wallet and gave Alicia a ticket as well.

"Oh, Alex, I just know you're going to the NFL, honey. You've done the unthinkable already, and it's only your freshman year," said Granny.

"I think I'll make it too, Granny," he replied.

"Just be careful of those gold-digging girls! They'll do anything to get in your pocket, baby," the old woman said.

Alicia looked at Alex. Granny's words made her wonder whether Alex was cheating on her in college. A sad frown appeared on her face.

The Rose Bowl arrived in the blink of an eye. The Michigan State Spartans vs the Oregon Ducks was going to be a good game to watch. Thousands of people were present at the ultimate college game of the year. Beautiful cheerleaders from both teams were dancing and shaking their colorful pom-poms. It didn't take long for the game to begin.

Michigan State received the ball at the starting kickoff. Alex was on the sideline with his helmet in hand, prepared to go quarterback. He gazed behind him into the crowd and saw his granny, his uncle Alvin, and Alicia sitting together. Alicia waved to him. Alex smiled as he waved back at her.

The kickoff returner for Michigan State caught the ball as it came flying from the other side of the field. He caught the ball at the ten yard line and dashed away running. He was tackled after running a few yards. As the Michigan State's offense ran on to the field, the commentators bolstered Alex's name over the loud speaker.

"And into the game comes the undefeated Michigan State offense and the amazing AR-15! For those who of you who don't know, AR-15 stands for Alex Revere, number 15," said Charlie.

"Well, Charlie, This is going to be a really good game. But if I had to bet ten thousand dollars, I'd put my money on that darn AR-15! The kids truly has an arm like an assault rifle," said George, laughing.

"Well, George. Don't count Oregon out. This is definitely going to be a great bowl game," said Charlie.

The game began again right as the commentators were done voicing their opinions.

Alex stood behind his offensive line examining everything. He touched the top of his helmet, then yelled, *"Hike!"*

The center tossed the ball backward between his legs to Alex. Alex quickly handed the football to the running back and gave him a chance to run. Michigan State lost three yards on the rushing play. Alex decided to throw the ball the next play to prove a point. He reset quickly. The team lined up again in the same formation.

"Down, set, hike!" yelled Alex. He grabbed the ball and started stepping backward. After four seconds he threw a long Hail Mary to Cody Harris. Cody had taken off running on a straight path, leaving his defensive opponent far behind him.

Cody managed to catch the sixty-yard pass but was tackled as soon as he caught it by the safety. Michigan State fans were celebrating in the crowd. The Spartans were now on the twenty yard line, closing in quickly on a touchdown. After Alex yelled *"Hike,"* he was rushed by a defensive tackle.

Alex was hit very hard and was sacked before he could do anything with the ball. Alex laid on the ground for a moment. When Alex didn't get up. Several people ran onto the field to assist him. The commentators began speaking their opinions loudly.

"Looks like the amazing AR-15 may be hurt," said Charlie.

After a minute, Alex stood up and shook it off. "I think I'll be all right," he said.

A lot of people were panicking, not knowing Alex's condition. Some envious people were being spiteful and hoping the Spartan quarterback was serious hurt! However, many fans were hoping and praying that Alex Revere was all right.

On second down, Alex was rushed and nearly sacked again. He had no choice but to throw the ball away, and the tackle hit him immediately after. A referee blew his whistle and threw a flag. The call was ruled as a late hit and roughing the passer. Alex was slightly upset on the next play. He screamed *"Hike!"* and threw a quick touchdown pass to Cody. The fans began celebrating in the stadium. The Spartan cheerleaders began cheering, and Cody did a quick dance move in the end zone. Afterward the Spartans kicked the field goal, making the score 7–0.

When the Oregon Ducks received the ball, they scored quickly, changing the score to 7–7.

When Michigan State got the ball back, they scored again. The score was now 14–7.

Apparently the Oregon Ducks were there to win because as soon as they received the ball again, they scored in three minutes tying the game up at 14–14. The two great teams battled back and forth, scoring touchdown after touchdown until halftime. Both teams had scored two touchdowns in the first quarter and two in the second quarter. The score at halftime was 28–28.

The coach of the Oregon Ducks envied Alex Revere's excellent quarterbacking. He was in the locker room speaking evil upon Alex.

"Hurt that quarterback! If you can bring down Alex Revere, you will automatically win this bowl game," the Ducks' coach said. Several players nodded at the coach, letting him know they completely understood.

It seemed like a short halftime break because the game resumed quickly. Oregon received the ball first after the halftime break. It was no surprise when they scored in four minutes, changing the score to 35–28. Michigan State was now down. The Ducks kicked the ball off long and hard to the other side of the football field. Mark Ronalton caught the ball and ran to the forty-four yard line before getting tackled.

During the first play Alex was rushed by a defensive tackle. He quickly threw the ball for a five-yard pass and was knocked down by the rusher. On second down with five yards to go, Alex was sacked and lost five yards. On third and ten, Alex quickly threw the ball to Cody. The ball hit him right in the chest, and he dropped it. The crowd screamed out, "Ohhhhh!" Alex placed both of hands on top of his helmet, filled with disbelief.

Cody was very disappointed in himself. Alex put his head down, took his helmet off, and trotted off the field. The punter for the Michigan State Spartans punted the ball long and hard. Their opponents caught the ball, and the runner took off at full speed—like a cheetah. He stiff-armed two people, and his blocker protected him flawlessly. Number 31 continued running full speed like he was unstoppable. He ran the ball all the way back from the punt return and scored a touchdown.

The Ducks' fans and cheerleaders began celebrating outrageously. After the one-point field goal, the score was 42–28. Suddenly, Michigan State was losing badly.

"George! Those Spartans are under a lot of pressure! Their offense is no match for the Ducks defense," said Charlie.

"I don't know, Charlie. There's still time left in the third quarter. Michigan State still has a chance," George replied.

When Alex got the ball back in his hands, he began throwing it like the best quarterback they'd ever seen. He was getting rid of the ball quickly by throwing short passes. All of the throws were complete, pass after pass. Michigan State managed to score again right at the end of the third quarter.

Unfortunately their opponents scored again at the beginning of the fourth quarter. Luckily it was only a three-point field goal. The score was now 45–35. It took Alex seven minutes to score on the next drive. By throwing short quick passes, it took more time than usual. However, Alex got the job done, making the score 45–42. Now Michigan State's defense had to step up and stop the Ducks from scoring another touchdown, and they did—but the Ducks kicked a field goal, putting three more points on the board. The score was now 48–42, and Michigan State was still losing by six points.

Two minutes were left on the clock. Alex knew he didn't have a lot of time. During a quick huddle, Alex informed the team of what his next three plays would be. They all agreed and understood the game plan. The Spartans were in horrible field position because their runner was tackled at the fourteen yard line after the kickoff. As Alex screamed, "*Hike!*" the clock began ticking. Alex dropped back in the pocket. After three seconds of examining the field, a rusher attacked him, but Alex refused to throw the ball away. He dashed to his right, scrambling like eggs. The rusher grabbed a piece of Alex's jersey but was unable to get him. As Alex made a run for it, everyone focused on the quarterback running. Cody continued running farther out, hoping Alex would see him, and he did.

While running to the right side, Alex spotted Cody and threw the ball long and hard right before he crossed the line of scrimmage. Alex bombed the ball a little too far, forcing Cody to dive sideways. Astonishingly Cody caught the seventy-yard pass as he fell to the ground, barely managing to hold onto the ball. The crowd went crazy!

Yelling, screaming, and cheering filled the stadium at the bowl game. Michigan State was now fifteen yards away. It was first down and goal. Alex hiked the ball quickly. A rusher broke through the offensive line and hit him extremely hard. When Alex didn't move, many different people rushed on the field again. When they asked him if he all right, he said, "No, coach! I can't keep playing. My right shoulder is killing me."

Alex was assisted as he hopped to the sideline. The third string quarterback went in to substitute for Alex. It was now second and goal with twenty-one yards to go because of the six-yard loss. The quarterback screamed "*Hike!*" The center passed the ball backward to him. The quarterback stepped backward in the pocket. He threw a bad pass on second down that fell incomplete.

Everybody was worried s the bowl game was on the line. The third string quarterback had very little experience. On third down, the pass was almost intercepted by the opponents, but the defender dropped it. It was now fourth and goal. Fifty-eight seconds were left in the game, and the score was 48–42.

"Timeout!" shouted the Michigan State coach.

The offense players ran off the field over to the sideline. "Coach, we need Alex for this last play of the game!" said an offensive lineman.

"Alex is hurt! We have to do the best we can and score right here. It's now or never! I need a twenty-one yards!" the coach yelled.

Cody disagreed and walked away from the huddle. He jogged over to Alex and begged him to at least try to come in for the last play. "Alex, we've been friends for years, bro! This bowl game means the world to me. If you're able, *please* get back in the game," he said desperately.

"All right, Cody. I'll try," said Alex.

"Coach! Alex is going to try this last play," said Cody.

Alex stood up. The coach looked at him. "Are you sure Alex?" he asked.

"Yeah, coach. I'm sure!" Alex replied.

The team ran onto the field, and Alex was the last one on. The crowd, cheerleaders, and fans began clapping and celebrating outrageously.

The announcers began screaming with surprise. "And would you look at this? Michigan State's quarterback, Alex Revere, is coming back on the field!" Charlie shouted.

"It's fourth down, Charlie, with twenty-one yards to go for the touchdown. AR-15 has to throw a touchdown pass right here! Right now! Or they lose the Rose bowl game!" said George.

"Down, set, hike!" shouted Alex. Alex stepped back, stumbled, and fell to the ground. The crowd cried out. A defensive player grabbed Alex before he had the opportunity to get back up. The game was lost, blown, and over. It appeared the Spartans had made a big mistake.

Out of nowhere, the referee blew the whistle. "Approachment! Defense, number 58! Ten-yard penalty! Michigan State ball. First down and goal!" shouted the referee.

The refs replayed the entire play and proved where number 56 was offsides to show they were not just cheating for the Spartans.

"Alex this may be the last chance!" said Cody seriously.

"I got us this time, bro! Just be ready. It's coming right before your eyes," whispered AR-15.

Michigan State was only eleven yards away from the end zone after the penalty.

"Down, set, hike!" shouted AR-15. Alex stepped backward into the pocket. He glanced around the field for three seconds and ran to his right side as he spotted Cody. He was rushed and forced to throw the ball.

The pass came right in front of Cody's face mask. He reached out, caught the eleven-yard touchdown pass, and held the ball up in the air triumphantly.

"Touchdown, Spartans!" shouted the commentator Charlie.

"AR-15 has done it again!" shouted the other commentator George.

Alex was smiling happily, and Cody was crying. He thanked God verbally, tossed the ball to the side, and dashed over toward Alex. Cody hugged Alex as he took off his helmet.

"You did it, bro! You did it!" said Cody, crying.

"No, Cody! *We* did it, bro," replied Alex, smiling.

Later there was a big celebration. It was no surprise that Alex was given the Heisman trophy. It was the first time Michigan State had gone undefeated and won the Rose Bowl. Alex had done the unthinkable. AR-15 was all over the newspaper. The nineteen-year-old quarterback was the best passer NFL scouts had ever seen.

The following week on Monday, January 14, 2019, Alex had a meeting with Bill Bailey. Bill was a multi-million-dollar businessman from Las Vegas, who was also great friends with the NFL Commissioner.

"Alex, the NFL laws are changing for next season. After one year of college football, you can be drafted if you are a Heisman trophy winner. You can now be drafted to the NFL. Now listen, kid. Every damn team in the NFL wants you. But I must ask, is there any specific team you want to play for? Because if there is, I can sure as hell get you on it," Bill said seriously.

Alex quietly contemplated. "Either the Detroit Lions, the Houston Texans, or the Cleveland Browns," replied Alex.

Bill spit three sunflower seeds on the floor intentionally. "Are you nuts, kid?! None of those teams have ever even won a Super Bowl!" he exclaimed.

"I know, sir! That's the reason I want to play for one of those three," replied Alex.

"Hell, the Miami Dolphins and the Kansas City Chiefs haven't won a Super Bowl in almost fifty years! I want to see one of them win. But if Detroit, Houston, or Cleveland is where you want to go. Then I'll be more than happy to make sure you're the starting quarterback for one of those teams," said Bill.

"Thanks, Mr. Bailey," said Alex. The two men stood up, shook hands, and went their separate ways.

Afterward Bill began calling each of the three teams Alex had mentioned. Propositions were being made, and deals were being agreed to; laws were being changed, and major rules were being bent. Alex Revere proved that a talented freshman college football player could make a big difference to the NFL game. He was the reason the rules were being modified.

Four months flew by, and the NFL draft came about before Alex even realized it. There were some teams with draft picks before Detroit, Houston, and Cleveland.

The Lions had the number three draft pick and picked Alex Revere first. It was very weird that the first two NFL teams did not bother picking Alex, but it would later be found out that every team in the NFL was commanded not to choose Alex Revere outside of three. Some higher officials of the NFL had given the Houston Texans, Detroit Lion and the Cleveland Browns the first shot at picking the young quarterback. Alex would be staying in Michigan and playing for Detroit.

There was a big party in Detroit for Alex after he was drafted to the Detroit Lions. A lot of the older guys were partying and drinking heavily because most of the people and players were over twenty-one.

Alicia showed up to the party, looking gorgeous. Alex was mesmerized instantly when he saw her. They began talking, laughing, and enjoying one another's company. Later Alexus showed up to the party looking for Alex; however, by the time she arrived, Alex had already left with Alicia.

Alex was genuinely in love with Alicia. She was his first love and his high school sweetheart. Although he was sexually obsessed with Alexus, he didn't want either of them to catch him with the other girl.

Alexus expected Alex to be at the party and was very disappointed when she didn't find him there. Some guy approached Alexus and tried to have a conversation with her. When she acted like she was uninterested in him, the guy told her that her boyfriend Alex had left with another young woman. This information made Alexus furious.

Alex and Alicia went out to dinner together that evening. They continued staring in each other's eyes, and smiling as they ate.

"Alex, do you still love me like you used to?" Alicia asked seriously.

"What? Of course, Alicia! Why would you ask such a thing?" replied Alex.

"Because, Alex, since you've been in college, we barely ever talk or hang out anymore," she said. Alicia paused for a second. Then she continued speaking. "I'm starting to feel like you've moved on."

Alex thought about all the cheating he had done in college. "Alicia, I love you, baby. I will never move on," replied Alex. The words made Alicia smile. "Just because I'm drafted to the NFL now, my love for you won't change. Alicia, look at me," he said. Alicia glanced up, gazing into Alex's amazing eyes. "No matter what—you will always be my number-one girl," Alex promised, smiling.

She smiled back and replied, "Well then, can we at least spend more time together?"

Alex smiled. "OK, Alicia. And since I'm right in Detroit, I want you to be at all my games too!"

"I would love to!" she replied happily.

The two of them began making out at the restaurant's table. After the intense kiss, Alicia laughed and said, "I miss being with you!"

SIX

AR-15 and the Lions

THE FIRST WEEK OF SEPTEMBER CAME QUICKLY, AND THE NFL regular season began. The Detroit Lions first game was against the Dallas Cowboys. Since the game was at home in Detroit, Alicia and Granny were both there in the front row.

Alex was standing in the locker room. He put on the 2017 number 12 Brady jersey that had come up missing at Super Bowl 51. Alex rubbed both of his hands on the jersey and spoke to it silently. *We've made it this far together. Let's see if we can go undefeated and make it to a real bowl game.* Alex then put on his helmet, shoulder pads, and other equipment. Within a few minutes, he was running out onto the field with all the players.

The commentators voiced their opinions. "Troy, this is going to be a great game! I've been waiting to watch this Alex Revere kid, who they call AR-15, throw the NFL football since he was drafted by the Lions back in May," said Bob.

"I agree with you, Bob! Alex Revere went undefeated all season at Michigan State his freshman year. The kid won the Rose Bowl and the Heisman trophy. I mean, the Detroit Lions have that special quarterback they've been waiting for," said Troy.

The first game of the season kicked off, and Dallas scored the first touchdown. When the Lions received the ball, AR-15 threw twelve complete passes in a row and scored a quick touchdown. The players, fans, and cheerleaders were all yelling and celebrating.

The score was now 7–7. Dallas had a good drive, and their offense scored another touchdown.

When the Detroit Lions got the ball back, Alex threw another twelve completions. The Lions made the touchdown on the twelfth throw and changed the score to 14–14.

By halftime, the score was 21–21. Alex had already thrown thirty-six complete passes out of thirty-eight attempts. After halftime, the Lions' defense stepped up and shut down the Dallas Cowboys' offense. When Alex got the ball, he threw ten more complete passes out of fourteen, and the Lions scored the touchdown. The score was now 28–21, Detroit was winning.

The commentators made a loud announcement. "Ladies and gentlemen, AR-15 has done it again! He has just broken the twenty-five-year-old NFL record previously held by Drew Bledsoe. In 1994 Drew Bledsoe had forty-five complete passes in one game, but Alex Revere has surpassed that record with forty-six!"

"And there's still time left in the fourth quarter. It's a good possibility that AR-15 will have at least a few more passes," said Bob.

The Lions defense prevented the Cowboys from scoring any more points at all. The final score was 31–21. The Dallas Cowboys had lost to AR-15 and the Detroit Lions.

Alex threw forty-nine complete passes that day.

Game two came quickly. The Lions had to go to Louisiana to play New Orleans Saints. Since the game was an away game, Alicia, David, and Granny watched the game on television together.

The Lions received the ball first. In this particular game, Alex was throwing the ball like never before. He was throwing long passes back-to-back to his receivers, and they were catching them.

His very first play, Alex threw a forty-four yard complete pass. Then he threw a forty-two-yard complete pass for a touchdown.

Later Alex threw a sixty-three-yard pass. Another time in the third quarter Alex bombed an eighty-nine-yard complete pass. Then he threw a Hail Mary in the beginning of the fourth quarter. It was a ninety-two-yard complete pass. Although he never hit the record of throwing the ninety-nine yard pass, Alex had already thrown for over five hundred yards that game. It was now the fourth quarter, and three minutes remained on the clock. The score was 48–30, and the Lions were winning. Alex Revere had thrown for 544 yards. The nineteen year old was on his way to breaking another record.

"Troy, I must say Brees is doing an excellent job of throwing that ball, but AR-15 is on fire!" said Bob.

"Honestly, Bob, I want the Saints to hurry up and score so Alex Revere can throw for at least eleven more yards to break the sixty-seven-year-old record," said Troy.

The New Orleans Saints were driving the ball. They managed to get way down the field but were forced to kick a field goal. The Saints were down eighteen points. It was inevitable they would lose this game, with two minutes now left to go on the clock.

The field goal was good, changing the score to 48–33.

At the two minute warning, the referees blew their whistles. The football game was stopped for a break. Shortly after, the game resumed, and Alex threw a nice pass to one of his receivers for a twenty-two yard gain.

The commentators made a loud announcement that AR-15 had thrown for 566 yards this game, breaking the sixty-seven-year-old record, previously held by Norman Van Brocklin, who had thrown for 554 yards in a game way back in 1951.

"Troy, this kid is God's gift to football, man!" shouted Bob.

"I have no choice but to agree, Bob. He's amazing! He must have a rabbit foot underneath that number 15 jersey of his," said Troy

"Yeah! Either that or a lucky Peyton Manning jersey mixed with a Tom Brady jersey underneath there," said Bob, laughing.

Alex threw a long pass on second down with one minute left in the fourth quarter. The safety on the New Orleans Saints intercepted the ball.

The safety managed to get help from his teammates with blocking. He stiff-armed a player on the Lions and ran in for the touchdown. The score quickly changed to 48–40 after the extra point was good.

The Saints did an onside kick to Detroit, but the Lions recovered the football. Alex knelt the ball on the first down with forty-eight seconds left on the clock. The game was genuinely over with. Alex would only kneel the ball again and watch the clock wind down to zero. The Detroit Lions began celebrating for the win at the Mercedes-Benz Superdome.

The TV reporter spoke to Alex after the victorious game about his new record in the NFL. The female reporter held the microphone up near Alex's mouth and asked, "How did you accomplish so many passing yards in one game?"

"Well, first, I must thank God because without him, none of this would be possible for me to accomplish. I must congratulate my teammates because without the offensive line, I wouldn't have the need to throw the ball or the long passes. I also must thank my receivers for catching my throws, because without them catching my balls, I wouldn't have thrown for 566 yards tonight. It feels good to break Norman Van Brocklin's record. So like I say, it's teamwork. Team effort. And there's a good chance you'll see us in the playoffs," said Alex, smiling.

"Also, Revere! There's been a lot of talk about the amazing AR-15 being the one who will take the Lions to their first Super Bowl victory," said Sandra, the black female reporter.

"Well, I know there's a lot of great talent out there, and I love my team and players. But it's way too early in the season to say such a beautiful thing. We'll play one game at a time. And if we make it that far, that will be a blessing," said Alex.

"Well, ladies and gentlemen, you heard it from Alex Revere yourself! Thank you, Alex!" said the reporter. Alex nodded at the lady and walked away.

The players snuck up from behind and poured a big cooler filled with orange Gatorade on Alex. He looked down. Luckily he'd taken of his jerseys.

⇨

Alex met Alexus when he returned to Detroit. He went to her apartment to cuddle and spend time with her. The two of them were laughing, playing, and kissing one another every other minute. They sat in the living room watching the movie *Frogged-Man: The 7ᵗʰ Humanimal*. After a while Alex got up and went to the bathroom. He left his cell phone behind on the sofa.

Alexus watched him closely as he walked to the bathroom. Once he'd shut the bathroom door, she reached over and grabbed his cell phone. She used an app from her phone to unlock the hidden secrets of Alex's. Alexus started scrolling through his cell phone, and she began gasping immediately. Her mouth opened wide as she saw pictures of Alicia kissing Alex and photos of other nude women. She opened text messages and began reading them. From the text messages that read: *I love you; I miss you;* and *we are going to get married one day*, Alexus realized that Alex was sincerely in love with some girl named Alicia.

Alexus started crying with the phone in her hand. She began to shake, shiver, and cough as she cried very hard. It was plain to see she was extremely hurt by the pictures and text messages in Alex's I-phone.

As Alex came out of the bathroom, he saw her crying and cried out. "Alexus! What's wrong?"

She gave him a hateful look, with the phone in her hand. "What's wrong? This is what's wrong!" she shouted, throwing his phone at him.

Alex caught the phone and began looking at the same pictures and texts Alexus had seen. Alexus had tears rolling down out of her eyes.

"So you're in love with somebody else! Y'all are going to get married one day!" shouted Alexus, who was extremely mad.

"Listen, Alexus—" Alex began.

Alexus cut him off, shouting, "No, Alex! Just get out!"

Alex walked toward her, trying to apologize and compromise. Alexus pushed him away from her, and Alex dropped his phone. Alexus quickly picked up the phone and slung it against the wall, smashing into pieces.

"Get out! I hate you! You're cheating on me!" Alexus shouted.

"Alexus! Would you please just listen? Let me explain!" Alex shouted back.

"Explain? There's nothing to explain! You're a lying piece of shit, Alex!" Alexus said.

Alex looked at her and put both of his hands up. "OK then! If that's how you feel, maybe I will marry her—and we'll be rich and live happily ever after," shouted Alex.

As soon as he said the words, Alexus slapped Alex in the face very hard. He put his left hand up to soothe the pain, looked at her, and said, "I'm done with you, Alexus!"

He turned around and began walking toward the front door of the apartment. As Alex turned his back, Alexus ran up and began pushing him, trying to push force him toward the door faster.

"I'm leaving, Alexus! Get your hands off of me!" shouted Alex. As he reached behind him to swipe her hands off of his back, his left elbow hit Alexus in the mouth.

She stumbled backward holding her mouth. Alex looked back at her, staring for a moment. He decided not to reenter the home. Alex walked out of the front door and left to avoid a worse altercation. Alexus looked up at the blinking red light on the camera near the ceiling, realizing it had witnessed the entire incident.

Alexus contemplated that night. Then she called the police the next day. She told the police that Alex Revere had hit her in the mouth and busted her lip. The cops took pictures of her face to verify the big split in her lip that had recently occurred, but Alexus did not give the cops the video footage of the incident. She knew it would show her as the aggressor.

Later that day, the cops showed up to Granny's house looking for Alex, but he was in Phoenix. He had only been in town for two days before having to fly out to play against the Arizona Cardinals.

Alex had to clear his mind and stay focused. His third game with the Detroit Lions was his priority. He knew the Cardinals had a great defense, and Larry Fitzgerald at wide receiver would be a big threat also.

Game three: Detroit Lions vs Arizona Cardinals

The game wasn't as hard as Alex expected it to be. He put the number twelve New England jersey on and went to work. With Tom Brady's missing Super Bowl jersey on, Alex was a true gunslinger. The running back was very disappointed with Alex, only did one running play the whole entire game, allowing the running back eight rushing yards total. The final score was 66–14. The name Alex Revere made the front cover of *USA Today*, the *Phoenix Republic*, and every newspaper in Michigan.

Alex had broken another NFL record. He'd thrown for nine touchdowns in one game, which had never been done in the NFL before. Alex was astounded by the unbelievable score of 66–14. The Detroit Lions had done it again. Three games in a row, Alex Revere had broken some serious NFL records.

Alex was well aware that a warrant had been issued for his arrest in Michigan. He had intentions to turn himself in when he returned to his home state. Unfortunately, Alex was arrested as soon as he walked off the plane in Detroit. The officers read him his rights and placed him in handcuffs. One police officer escorted Alex to the back seat of a squad car and locked him in the back seat. Alex was extremely sad as the police car drove him away. He peeked up front and noticed the officer had at least grabbed his luggage and brought it along. When they arrived to the jail, he called Granny and Alicia to come bond him out. He didn't have any cash on his person.

Granny and Alicia rushed to go pay a bondsman the required amount. Not long afterward Alex was released, never even having to go to a real jail cell. When Granny and Alicia arrived to pick him up. Alex was very silent. He sat in the backseat, feeling dejected. Alicia sat in the passenger seat, thinking.

As the three of them drove away in Granny's car, Alicia spoke up. "What happened for you to be charged with domestic violence on some girl?"

"I didn't do anything wrong, OK? I'd rather not even talk about it. I'll go hire a lawyer tomorrow and try and get all of this cleared up, Alex said.

Granny looked over at Alicia in the passenger seat before glancing sadly in her rearview mirror at Alex.

"Well, Alex, I must say one thing," said Granny wisely.

"What is it, Granny?" asked Alex, softly and respectfully.

"Whoever she is, stay away from her, Alex. You are a professional football star now. Things like this can ruin your career and everything you've worked so hard to achieve."

"I know, Granny," said Alex politely.

She spoke one last time. "Alex, you're twenty years old. You're probably one of the youngest people in the NFL—"

"I am the youngest." Alex interrupted her.

"Well, Alex, you are a target. You're young, you're handsome, and if you continue prospering at everything you do, you'll be wealthy, son. If I don't get to tell you nothing else, remember this: The greatest natural resource is your youth, son. Cherish it. The greatest loss is the loss of self-respect, and the most crippling disease is excuses. Rather you did it or didn't do it. Stay away from her for good. And don't do it again. Understand?" said Granny, her eyes firmly on the road.

"Yes, ma'am, Granny," said Alex respectfully. Alex loved and respected his granny. When she spoke, he listened. When she yelled, he quieted himself, and when she told him to do something, he never argued, he just *did* it.

The next day Alex was all over the news and on the front page of the Michigan newspaper. Everyone was gossiping about his domestic violence accusations. His NFL coach called a press conference and spoke to the media concerning the situation.

Alex, who was was at a lawyer's office watching the news with his attorney, listened to his coach speak and defend him on national television.

"My quarterback, Alex Revere, is a great young man and an outstanding athlete. He has amazing characteristics, and I do not believe he committed such a crime. I believe the accusations of domestic violence are false. However, if Alex is guilty of such actions the team owner and NFL commissioner will make sure the proper and necessary punishment is executed. I ask that fans of Alex Revere and the Detroit Lions not just jump to conclusions until this matter is genuinely investigated and resolved," the coach said.

"Thank you, Coach, for speaking with us.," said the female news reporter. The coach nodded and departed.

Alex focused on the lawyer sitting at the desk. The attorney picked up the remote control and turned the television off. "Have a seat, Alex," he said.

Alex sat down in the chair directly in front of the desk. The lawyer looked deeply into Alex's eyes and spoke again. "Son, listen—the NFL takes domestic violence charges extremely seriously, especially since what happened with Ray Rice and the Baltimore Ravens. Rice was caught on videotape assaulting his spouse."

"I know, Mr. Eisenmenger," replied Alex.

"Be honest with me, kid. Did you do it?"

"No! I mean—this is what happened ..." Alex began speaking and explained every little detail of what had occurred that evening between him and Alexus. After listening, the attorney rubbed his chin.

"So what do you think?" Alex asked curiously.

"I think you have a good chance at winning this. I just wish there was someone who witnessed the whole incident," said the lawyer.

"But no one else was there but me and her."

"That's what makes it a good case. It's her word versus your word. It's not like you were caught on camera beating her up," said the lawyer.

"That's it! The camera! There's a camera in her apartment, right by the door. The camera had to have recorded everything that happened. If you can get that video footage, it would prove I'm innocent!" Alex shouted, smiling.

"Really?" said the lawyer.

"Yes."

"Honestly, kid, I thought your story was fabricated. Most men hit women and make an excuse."

"No, sir! That's not the case here."

"Well, Alex, if the story you gave me is genuine and was caught on camera, a lot of people are going to look stupid for criticizing you," said the lawyer.

"Will you be able to get the video recording?" asked Alex.

"If it's one in her home, you can bet a million bucks I'm going to get it. But it may take some time," said the lawyer.

"Yes! Thank you so much, sir!" said Alex. The two men shook hands over the desk.

"You're welcome, Alex! Good luck in the NFL," replied the attorney.

Alex drove around Detroit for a while in his new white Bentley Flying Spur. After he was done cruising around the city, he went to Granny's house. He parked the luxurious car and exited. When he entered the home, he noticed no one was there.

Alex began looking around at trophies and pictures that brought back vivid memories. He saw a picture of him with his mother and father before they'd died. Alex picked up the picture and kissed it. He walked over to a picture of him and his teammates at the high school championship game. Alex smiled to himself at the memory. He glanced over at another picture of him and Cody together at the Rose Bowl, hugging each other after their flawless victory and undefeated season at Michigan State.

He saw another picture of him holding his Heisman Trophy in college. Alex picked up the picture and admired it. Then he picked up a photo of him and his beautiful biracial princess, Alicia, together on prom night. Granny had numerous old pictures that brought back vivid, lovely memories to Alex. He was dumbfounded when he saw a black and white picture, browned with age, of a strong-looking older man. Alex picked up the picture.

"Who is this man?" Alex whispered.

"That's my great-great-grandfather Paul Revere with his grandson," a voice said. Alex had been so absorbed in the pictures, he hadn't heard Granny come in.

"Granny! You scared me. I didn't know anyone was here," said Alex.

"Yeah, well I'm here. My car is in the shop. That's why you didn't see it out front. What did the lawyer say?" she asked.

"Oh, he says he's going to get the video evidence to prove I'm innocent, but it's going to take time," said Alex.

"Well that's good then, son."

SEVEN

The NFL Playoffs

T HE NEXT TWELVE WEEKS OF THE PROFESSIONAL FOOTBALL SEASON flew by. Week after week, Alex and the Detroit Lions defeated their opponents. From game four to game fifteen the Lions were victorious. With AR-15 in charge, the games weren't difficult for their team.

Game sixteen, however, was a greater challenge for AR-15 and the Lions. At 7:15 p.m. the final game of the regular season began. The commentators began talking and giving an introduction before the game kicked off.

"Chuck, tonight is going to be a great game! We have the flawless Detroit Lions who haven't lost a game all season versus the great New York Giants," said Troy.

"Listen, Troy, I admire the young, amazing AR-15 and the way he throws the ball, but I'm from New York City. I love my Giants! We've done great this season with a thirteen and two record. I'm putting my bets with Eli Manning and the Giants," said Chuck seriously.

"Well, Chuck, get ready to lose your bet, because AR-15 and those kings of the jungle are truly the best NFL team in America right now. Alex Revere has thrown forty-nine touchdown passes this season already, as a rookie quarterback. If he throws six or seven more in this game, he could either tie or break Peyton Manning's 2013 record of throwing fifty-five touchdown passes in one season," said Troy.

"And yes, Troy, I must concur. Alex Revere is definitely the best rookie quarterback of all time. I admire the records he has broken. But my Giants have won consecutive Super Bowl victories. Neither AR-15, nor the Lions, have ever won the big game, so I'll leave it at that," Chuck said sarcastically.

The game was relatively simple. Each team scored two touchdowns in the first quarter and two in the second. The score was 28–28 at halftime. In the third quarter the Lions scored one touchdown, and the Giants didn't score at all.

The fourth quarter came and the score was 35–28. The Giants had an awful drive and had to punt the ball to the Lions. In less than a minute Alex Revere took full advantage of the opportunity and scored another touchdown. The Lions went up two touchdowns. The score was now 42–28. The Lions kicked the ball off to the New York Giants with eleven minutes and twenty-nine seconds left.

It took the Giants six minutes and twenty-one seconds to score a touchdown. The score was now 42–35, and the Lions were still up. When AR-15 and the Detroit Lions got the ball back, they had a nice three minute and four seconds drive; however, they only managed to accomplish a three-point field goal. The score was now 45–35 with exactly two minutes and four seconds left on the clock.

With great motivation and excellent ambition, Eli Manning began throwing the ball like the two-time Super Bowl champion he was. He scored the touchdown in less than one minute—fifty-six seconds to be precise. He'd only thrown four complete passes: two long ones to the outstanding Odell Beckham Jr. and two to a new rookie receiver.

Beckham caught an amazing one-hand touchdown pass, changing the score to 45–42 after the extra point. Amazingly, there was still one minute and eight seconds left on the clock. Instead of kneeling the ball, Alex threw a long pass that was intercepted at the fifty yard line. He was desperately trying to achieve another passing touchdown. The interceptor ran six yards back before being tackled.

With fifty-three seconds left in the game, the Giants fans began celebrating. There was hope and a good chance they could still win the game. After the interception, Eli Manning came into the game on offense. He began showing them why he was one of the very few quarterbacks in history to have two Super Bowl MVPs.

He threw three quick passes. The great Odell Beckham Jr. caught the fourth pass, which resulted in a touchdown. The crowd and fans at New York Giants stadium went crazy, celebrating and cheering. The score was now 45–49, and the Giants were on top.

"I told you, Troy!" shouted Chuck. "Touchdown, Giants!"

There were twenty-four seconds left on the clock, and the Lions were down by four. A touchdown was necessary to win the game. The kicker kicked off to the Lions, and the ball sailed all the way into the end zone, forcing the Lions to start at the twenty yard line. Alex entered the game with eyes on the touchdown.

"Come on," Alex whispered to his magical jersey. "We've been winning all season. Let's go undefeated again like we did together at Michigan State."

Alex called for the hike, stepped back, and threw the ball thirty-three yards to Tommy Thomas. Thomas ran two more yards and went out of bounds to stop the clock. They were now on their forty-five yard line. It was first and ten, with nineteen seconds left on the clock. Alex screamed hike, grabbed the ball, and quickly threw it to John Dixon.

Dixon caught the thirty-one-yard pass and ran toward the sideline. He gained eight yards before being tackled. With eight seconds left on the clock, the Lions called a timeout. They were now on the six yard line, closing in on a touchdown.

"Alex, we need a touchdown. We're in field goal range, but a field goal won't win it. Get that ball in that rectangle," said the coach.

"I got us, Coach," replied Alex, who was ready to go.

After the huddle, the team ran back on the field. The commentators spoke. "Chuck, those Lions are closing in on that touchdown. Alex Revere has tied the perfect Peyton Manning record with fifty-five touchdown passes this season. If he can throw one right here, he'll break another record," said Troy.

"Well, let's watch and see," replied Chuck.

Alex hiked for the ball, grabbed it, and stepped back behind his offensive line. Since the Lions were a passing team, they rarely utilized their running back, and the Giants' defensive coordinator was very surprised. Alex tossed the ball to Moses Jones, and the young running back dashed through a loophole. The powerful running back scored the touchdown with two seconds left on the clock. The Detroit fans went berserk. Screaming, cheering, clapping, and happiness filled the Giants' stadium.

"Touchdown, *Lions!*" shouted Troy.

The score was now 52–49 after the extra point attempt was successful. Alex had only tied the 2013 Peyton Manning record, but the Detroit Lions had sixteen wins and zero losses. They were undefeated and on their way to the playoffs. Since they had the best record in the NFL, the first week of the playoffs would be a bye week for them.

Alex was contacted by his lawyer right after that Monday night game. "Alex, I have the video of the fight between you and Alexus," said the attorney.

"Really?!" Alex exclaimed.

"Yes, I watched it myself. Tomorrow we're going before a judge for an exoneration hearing. I need you to be there," said the lawyer.

"Well, I'm in New York City right now, but I'll be there for the hearing," said Alex.

"Good! It's at nine o'clock in the morning! Dress casually. I'm sure a lot of news reporters and other nosy people are going to be there," he cautioned.

"OK, sir, I will."

"Also, congratulations on your flawless undefeated season with the Detroit Lions. You're an amazing quarterback. You remind me of the great Tom Brady in his prime," replied the lawyer.

Alex smiled widely at the comment. "Thanks, Mr. Eisenmenger."

"Well, Alex—Mr. AR-15—I'll see you in court tomorrow," said the attorney.

The next day the judge watched the video of the incident that proved Alex Revere was not the aggressor right in open court. The judge's final words were: "After watching and reviewing the audio and video of the domestic violence accusation, I find that Mr. Alex Revere is not guilty as charged. I also see that Mr. Revere put his hands up in the air after Ms. Alexus White intentionally slammed his nine hundred dollar cell phone against the wall, smashing it. He also walked away and was attacked again by Ms. White. And I notice he did not punch her in the mouth like the police report indicates she claimed happened. For all of these reasons, I am granting Mr. Alex Revere and his attorneys motion to exonerate. I'm dropping all charges in this case."

"Thank you, Your Honor," said Alex's attorney.

As Alex walked out of the courtroom, several reporters rushed up to question him. Alex's attorney didn't speak and refused to let him to speak either.

During the bye weekend, Alex sat at Granny's house eating Papa John's pizza and watching the games with Alicia and David. They watched as the New Orleans Saints won their playoff game and would be going to round two of the playoffs. Alex was well aware that the saints would be the team he would have to face and battle after the bye week was over.

The next week came very quickly, and the post-season action began. The Saints had to come to Detroit to play the Lions, since they were the best team in the NFC (National Football Conference). Without anything spectacular happening, the halftime score was 21–14. Plainly, the Saints were up a touchdown. The second half was relatively simple also. The Saints scored a touchdown and one field goal. The Lions scored three touchdowns—two in the third quarter and one in the fourth. The Lions won the game 35–31.

The next round of the playoffs came rapidly also. The Lions had the play the great Green Bay Packers in the NFC Championship Game. Fortunately Detroit's defense played their hardest the first half of the game, putting the quarterback for Green Bay under a lot of pressure. The score was 38–7 at the halftime, and Green Bay was losing tremendously.

At the beginning of the third quarter, Alex was rushed and sacked pretty hard. He fell on his right shoulder and laid there in pain. The nurses, trainers, and others ran onto the field and carried Alex to the sideline. His right shoulder was out of place, and the game had to resume without Alex. The backup quarterback who replaced Alex was trash. He was not a good replacement or comparison to AR-15. The Lions defense was tired already. The backup quarterback didn't complete many passes and didn't score at all in the third quarter; however, Aaron

Rogers and the Packers scored twice by the end of the third quarter. The score was 38–21. At the beginning of the fourth quarter, the Lions were still winning due to Alex's excellent performance in the first half while wearing his lucky number 12 jersey underneath. However, the backup was still throwing the football poorly.

He continued throwing incomplete pass after incomplete pass. Aaron Rogers continued capitalizing like the 2011 Super Bowl MVP and champion he was. By the two-minute warning, the Packers had scored two more touchdowns, making the score 38–35. The Packers were down by three. The Lions had another poor drive and punted the ball with one minute and 20 seconds left on the clock. The Packers saw an opportunity to win the game or at least tie it up.

"The Packers could score a touchdown and win the NFC Championship right here," said the commentator.

"Or at least tie it up and go to overtime," said Troy.

By the time the Packers got past midfield, there were sixteen seconds left on the clock. It was fourth and long. The offensive coordinator decided to try a sixty-four-yard field goal to try and tie the game up.

All eyes were on the field, and all eyes were on the kicker. This game would determine which team would go to the Super Bowl. The Packers were anxious for the shot they had right here to put it in overtime to win this NFC Championship Game. Every Green Bay Packer player, coach, and fan was sad and hurt when the kicker missed the field goal.

Lions' fans celebrated and cheers. The Green Bay Packers' coach wasn't mad. The team had made a tremendous, miraculous comeback, and had done well. A sixty-four-yard field goal was incredibly difficult, and the coordinators and coaches knew that.

"And the field goal is no good," said Troy.

"Well, Troy, a sixty-four-yard field goal is just about the longest one ever kicked. One that long has never been made in NFL history. I didn't expect him to make that one either," said Chuck.

"Neither did I! But it would've been great if he would have," said Troy.

The black female reporter walked over and spoke with Alex Revere as he was sitting on the sideline, injured. "Alex Revere, you and the Lions had the Packers down by thirty-one points at halftime. You had an excellent lead until you were hurt in the beginning of the third quarter. Then the Packers took advantage of that injury; however, the thirty-one point lead managed to stand up to the last minute, even though the backup quarterback was unable to put any more points up on the board. How do you feel now that you are going to the Super Bowl?"

"Well, honestly, I'm happy—because who would've thought we were really going to make it this far? I'm disappointed by my injury because it may take a few weeks to completely heal," said Alex sadly.

"Now you say it may take a few weeks to completely heal. Just for verification, the Super Bowl is exactly two weeks from now! Does that mean you will not be playing in the big game in February?" she asked curiously.

"Well, according to medical personnel I may be able to play in the Super Bowl. Depends on my condition," said Alex, tearing up.

"Do you think the Lions will be able to do it without you after what you saw tonight?" she asked.

Alex hesitated before saying, "Anything is possible!"

EIGHT

Half of a Super Bowl

ALTHOUGH IT WASN'T EXACTLY A SURPRISE TO ALEX, HIS GRANNY died on January 31, 2020. The young NFL quarterback was still extremely heartbroken by the loss, even though he'd known it was coming. Alex sat on the sofa talking to Alicia on his cell phone.

"I feel like all she really wanted was to see me play in the Super Bowl. When I got injured in the NFC Championship Game, it's like … she let go of life," Alex said, exhaling deeply into the phone.

"Alex, I could already tell she was barely hanging in there. She even said she was ready to go to a heavenly form. Try not to be sad, baby. The Super Bowl is in a few days. Your shoulder is doing much better. You have to stay focused," Alicia said, doing her best to inspire him.

"Yeah, I guess you're right. I just wanted her to be there for the big game, Alicia. I really wanted my granny to see me play in the Super Bowl," he said.

Alex and Alicia attended Granny's sad funeral that Saturday, which was only a day before the Super Bowl. A nice number of Alex's teammates, friends, and family attended. Alex was inconsolable and reluctant to communicate with anyone. He felt like his life was coming to an end—and he wasn't even twenty-one years old yet. His coach spoke briefly with him and gave him encouraging words during the funeral.

"Listen, Alex, we have the biggest game in Detroit Lions history tomorrow. You have to stay mentally focused kid. Do what your granny would have loved to see you do," Coach said. He paused for a moment, and Alex looked him deeply in the eyes. The coach smiled and spoke again. "I want to see you win that Super Bowl in Atlanta tomorrow!"

Alex smiled and said, "All right, Coach."

After the funeral was over, Alex and Alicia went home to Granny's house. Although some players caught a plane to Atlanta that evening, Alex's plane was scheduled to leave Sunday at noon. Alex and Alicia cuddled together watching television until they fell asleep.

The next day Alex and Alicia arrived to the Detroit Metropolitan Wayne County Airport at 11:00 a.m. They made it there on time as everyone was loading up on the airplane. As all the passengers were seated comfortably, there was an announcement that the plane was overcrowded. Seven people had to get off before the flight took off. A tall, male flight security officer approached Alex and Alicia. They glanced up at the man curiously, as he informed them that Alicia had to get off the plane.

Alex looked at the man angrily. "Sir! I have a Super Bowl game tonight in Atlanta! Do you have any idea who I am?" he asked seriously.

"Yes, Mr. Revere, I've been the manager of Detroit Metropolitan Airport for a decade. There's nothing I can do about it. The names are selected randomly, and your girlfriends name was chosen. She will have to catch the next flight," said the manager.

"Wow! This is unbelievable!" shouted Alex.

"Baby, calm down. It's all right. I'll just catch the next flight or watch the game from the house. It's no big deal," Alicia said kindly.

Alex inhaled deeply to release his frustration. "Come here baby!" said Alex, and the couple embraced one another. They hugged and kissed passionately while the airport manager and others observed.

"*Ahem.*" The manager cleared his throat to get their attention. "Mr. Revere, we have to go. The flight needs to leave."

The two lovers ceased their public display of affection and said their farewells. "Good luck, baby! Go win that Super Bowl for Granny!" Alicia said, smiling.

Alex winked and replied, "Trust me, baby. I will!"

"I love you, Alex," Alicia said.

He smiled. "I love you too, beautiful."

Alicia waved goodbye to her NFL-star boyfriend as she departed. Her eyes were watery as she exited the plane, but there was nothing Alex or she could do about it. She picked up her two bags of luggage and headed down the ramp as the plane Alex was on flew away without her.

Alicia went back in the airport to speak with the manager of the airlines. She found out that the next flight would be leaving at 6:00 p.m.

"I can't wait here for six more hours for a plane, sir. It's only twelve o'clock," said Alicia.

"Well, ma'am, it's either that or chose a different airline," he replied. Alicia decided to just go home and watch the game with her family.

She opened her luggage to search for her spare key to Alex's Bentley Flying Spur. She began pulling things out, looking for her purse.

This isn't even my luggage. This is Alex's stuff, she thought. She took a deep breath and continued to look for the key to the car. She pulled out the missing Super Bowl jersey with the number 12 on the back and a few other of Alex's belongings. She sat them to the side as she continued to look for the key, which it wasn't long before she found. She placed all of Alex's clothes back into the bag and headed for the car.

Alex landed in Atlanta, Georgia, and made it to the stadium around four o'clock. He greeted his fellow teammates, and they celebrated a little bit. The game wouldn't begin for another four hours, so the Lions began playing around and practicing with one another. It took a while before Alex realized the jersey was missing. He searched through his luggage and concluded he had one of Alicia's bags.

"Dammit! I don't have the jersey!" he shouted, worried. Alex began to panic before finally calling Alicia and explaining his situation. She'd had no idea the jersey was really divine or that Alex never played without it. When he told her to get on that next plane when it departed at 6:00 p.m., she agreed. Alex felt like Alicia would have enough time to fly to Atlanta from Detroit and get the jersey to him before the game was over. Until she arrived with the jersey, he would have to do the best he could.

The Detroit Lions were scheduled to play the Miami Dolphins at the Super Bowl in Atlanta. The Dolphins had a great team they'd built up over the last few years. They hadn't won the Super Bowl—nor been to one—since 1974. They were eagerly determined to defeat any team that won the NFC Championship.

After the coin toss at 8:15 p.m., the Dolphins received the ball first. They chose heads, and heads it was. The high-powered Miami Dolphins offense didn't hesitate to go down and strike. They scored a touchdown in less than three minutes. The extra point was good, and the score was 7–0.

Alex knew Alicia's plane wouldn't land in Atlanta before the game started because of the distance from Detroit. Bravely, Alex had put on his helmet and entered the Super Bowl game without his unique, magnificent number 12 2017 New England Patriots jersey.

He had never actually played a college or NFL game without it, and he knew it wouldn't be the same at all. Alex began throwing nice, short passes. He threw five in a row that got the Lions to almost midfield. His sixth pass was bad, and it was intercepted.

"Interception! AR-15 has thrown an interception on his first drive in this Super Bowl game!" shouted Chuck.

"Chuck, the Lions are off to a bad start already," said Troy.

Alex took off his helmet and walked off the field with his head down after the big mistake. The Miami Dolphins capitalized and scored another touchdown. After the extra point was good, the score changed to 14–0. There were still seven minutes left in the first quarter. When the Lions got the ball back, the team did a lot of running plays. The Lions' running back Moses Jones was happy. Since Alex had become their quarterback, he'd barely gotten to enjoy his position. Jones carried the ball like a great running back. He rushed forty-seven yards in that drive, managing to get the Lions in field goal range. The kick ended up being good, making the score 14–3.

The Dolphins received the ball, went downfield, and scored a quick touchdown, and their extra point was good as well. The Lions received the ball back with the score at 21–3. The Lions' defense was slacking. The first quarter ended and the second began.

Alex decided to use Moses Jones as much as he could. Although Jones wouldn't be able to do it alone, his legs were as powerful as an ox. Jones achieved great field goal position for the Lions once again. When Alex Revere failed to complete his passes, they were forced to kick another field goal at fourth down and ten to go. The kicker kicked the forty-nine yard field goal, and it was good. The score changed to 21–6. Unfortunately, the Lions didn't score any more points in the first half; however, the Dolphins scored another touchdown and two more three-point field goals. At halftime, the score was 34–6. The Detroit Lions were losing badly, and Alicia still hadn't arrived.

At halftime, the commentators, Chuck and Troy, voiced their opinions on the first half. "Well, Troy, I think those Lions you like so much have finally met their match. Their lethal weapon, AR-15, can't do anything to penetrate that strong Miami defense," said Chuck.

"I can't be in denial. Chuck, the Dolphins are playing great. I must congratulate them. But you have to remember Alex Revere hurt his shoulder two weeks ago in the NFC Championship Game. Since the injury, he hasn't been throwing accurately, but this game is not over, Chuck. We've seen teams losing like this who still come back and win," said Troy.

"No, Troy! No team has ever been down twenty-eight points in the Super Bowl and come back to win. The great Tom Brady made a miraculous comeback in Super Bowl 51 against the Atlanta Falcons, but you can't compare any other quarterback to Brady. Tom has five Super Bowl victories under his belt and four MVPs. No NFL player has ever accomplished what Brady has," said Chuck.

"Yes, Chuck, you're absolutely right. He's by far the greatest quarterback in the history of the NFL. That's unquestionable! I just believe any great quarterback can make a comeback under these circumstances, and from what I've seen Alex Revere accomplish, I know he has the potential to throw like Joe Montana, Tom Brady, or Terry Bradshaw used to. The kid has skills, Chuck," said Troy.

"Well, Troy, all three of those great quarterbacks have four Super Bowl victories, except for Brady, who has an extra. This kid has no rings. Yes, the records he has broken this year prove he has a God-given talent, but you and I both know the postseason is a different ball game," said Chuck. The two commentators spoke about other minor things, and then a beautiful young singer performed the halftime show, which was one of a kind—like nothing ever seen before.

Alex and the Lions were silent and depressed as they watched the show. They had done great all season. Many were disappointed that the team had done so well only to come to the Super Bowl to lose. Many Lions fans had already left the depressing game to avoid watching the inevitably losing battle. Alex began to cry as he wondered whether Alicia would make it there in time. He knew there was no AR-15 without Brady's Patriots jersey that had come up missing the first Sunday of February 2017 at Super Bowl 51.

After the halftime show ended, the coach came and spoke to Alex. "Alex, how are you kid?"

Alex wiped his eyes and replied, "I'm discouraged, Coach. I don't know what to do. I've never lost a college or NFL game before today."

"Alex, you listen to me! We can still win this game, kid. Detroit has never won a Super Bowl. You've brought us this far. Don't let us down here. Not now, son! You are our only hope. The team can't do it without you, kid. The moment you got hurt, everybody gave up, including me," said the coach. He paused and looked in Alex's eyes. "Alex, there are no Lions without AR-15. We're down twenty-eight points. I know you can still win this game. Do it for your granny, Alex. I know she's in heaven looking down, son."

Alex didn't reply. The coach patted him on the back and walked away. Alex glanced around, looking for Alicia, but she was nowhere to be found.

The Dolphins kicked the ball off to the Lions at the beginning of the third quarter. As the ball was kicked in the air, he heard his name being called by a feminine voice. "Alex!" shouted Alicia.

He looked up and saw Alicia running his way. He looked at her with his red, watery eyes and smiled. As she ran up to him, they hugged each other, kissed quickly, and smiled.

"Do you have the jersey?" Alex asked anxiously.

Alicia reached into her pink Chanel bag and pulled the number 12 Patriots jersey out of the bag. "You talking about this stinky jersey right here?" she asked coyly.

Alex smiled. "Thank you, baby! You're the best," Alex replied happily.

"You're welcome, baby! Now go win this Super Bowl!" she replied.

"Come on, Alex! We've got a game to win!" shouted the coach.

Alex put the jersey on in front of everyone and rushed onto the football field. Most of the fans had already given up hope and felt like the game was over. Alex brought the inspiration, motivation and enthusiasm that the Lions had been missing. The mystical Brady jersey took effect, sending a tingling feeling through Alex's body. Alex began slinging that football like a quarterback they'd never seen before, completing pass after pass after pass.

The Lions scored two touchdowns in the third quarter, and the Dolphins scored none. The Lions' defense was stepping up to the plate. The score was 34–20 at the end of the third quarter. The Dolphins quarterback fumbled the ball on the first drive of the fourth quarter. Alex didn't hesitate to throw seven excellent passes and scored again. The score was quickly 34–27. The Lions were still losing by seven. The Dolphins slowed things down a bit. Their quarterback began throwing short passes to extend the time used in their drive. The clock was winding down, and only four minutes remained. The Dolphins made a field goal attempt but missed. The score remained the same.

The Lions got the ball back and began driving down the field, when Alex suddenly threw an interception that devastate a lot of fans. Detroit's hopes of winning the Super Bowl went back down again. The Lions defense refused to give up or lay down at all. It made them play even harder with only three minutes and three seconds left on the clock. The Dolphins had three very hard downs and didn't get anywhere near field goal range. At fourth and seven yards to go, the Dolphins punted the ball back to the Lions.

There were two minutes and twelve seconds left on the clock. The ball went all the way into the end zone off the foot of the punter, so the Lions started at the twenty yard line. Alex put on his helmet and ran onto the field. He stood behind the offensive line, examining the field and the Dolphins' defensive set up. Then he had the football hiked to him. He started slinging like he'd been to the Super Bowl six times before. Alex showed no mercy and threw the ball perfectly. It was amazing how the football would pass right by a Dolphins' player and land in the hands of the Lions' receiver.

"This kid throws like he already has four rings!" shouted a man in the crowd.

With fifty-four seconds left in the fourth quarter, Alex moved the Lions into the red zone. They were twelve yards from the goal line, and it was first and goal.

Alex stood behind his offensive line and shouted, "Down! Set! *Hike!*"

A yellow flag was thrown by a referee as Alex slung the ball into the end zone. It was caught by a receiver, and the commentator yelled, "Touchdown! Lions!"

"Wait, Troy. I think it's a flag on Detroit," said Chuck.

The referee walked onto the field, raised his hands up, and spoke. "Offsides! Offsides! Number 88! Five-yard penalty! Second down and goal!"

The coach called a timeout. He was angry with number 88 and decided to take him out of the game. He had messed up the biggest play in the history of the Detroit Lions football organization.

"He's just nervous, Coach. Don't take him out of the game. I got this!" said Alex.

The coach let Alex make the final decision. All the players rushed back on the field. It was now second down. Alex examined the field first. Then he yelled, *"Hike!"* He stepped back and slung the ball to a receiver in the end zone, but the ball was a little too high for him to catch. It fell incomplete.

It was now third down and seventeen yards for the goal. There were twenty-eight seconds left on the clock. The score was still 34–27. Although they were in great field goal range, three points wouldn't cut it.

Alex tapped his helmet twice, examined the line, then yelled, "Hike! *Hike!*"

As a rusher blitzed him, Alex began scrambling like eggs. The referee threw the yellow flag again, but Alex continued running. The twenty-year-old, six-four quarterback stiff-armed a player on the Miami Dolphins defense and ran into the end zone, as the crowd began cheering as he scored the touchdown that could force overtime.

The ref ran onto the field and spoke. "Offsides! Offense! Number 88! Five-yard penalty! Fourth and goal! Twenty-two yards to go!"

A Detroit fan stood up and yelled, "Hell naw! Y'all cheating!"

The review of the play was showed on the big screen where number 88 had gone offsides again. The refs were not cheating. Alex slammed the football on the ground and was fortunate to not get penalized. He walked back behind the offensive line, disappointed. He had scored the touchdown twice in one minute and had been legally robbed.

"Chuck, I've never seen a Super Bowl ending as crazy as this one. AR-15 has put the ball in the end zone twice, and neither of them counted," said Troy seriously.

"Yeah, Troy! Number 88 is fired if they lose this game," said Chuck, laughing.

"Honestly! I think he's fired even if they do win," said Troy.

The game continued "Down! Set! Hike!" yelled Alex, standing behind the offensive line. He stepped back into the pocket. It seemed like everything was in slow motion. He looked around the field to see if anyone was open. He spotted John Dixion slanting across the the goal line with his hands out and open. Alex pulled his arm back and threw the ball with great force. The ball went full speed right into Dixion's palms, and he caught it and fell down in the end zone.

The refs lifted up both of their hands, the crowd began cheering, and the announcers yelled, "*Touchdownnnnnnnnnn, Lions!*"

They had not kicked the extra point yet, so the score was 34–33. The Miami Dolphins were still up by one point.

"I don't want to go to overtime, Coach! I want to win now! Let me put an end to this while I have the chance," said Alex.

"But, Alex, the two point conversion is too risky," said the Lions' coach.

"No it isn't, Coach! Trying to get all the way down the field to score again is more risky! I'm just a few yards away, Coach. Please let me try it. I promise I'm going to win this one for my granny!" said Alex.

A tear rolled down each of his cheeks. The coach looked into his watery eyes and saw the sincerity. "Go ahead, Alex! Show them why you're nicknamed AR-15," said the coach, smiling.

Alex smiled and nodded at the coach. He ran back onto the field. Before he hiked the ball, he looked up in the end zone. He did a double take when he saw, or thought he saw, four angels there cheering for him. "Mom! Dad! Granny! And ... my great-great-great-grandfather, Paul Revere," whispered Alex. He focused harder "Down! Set! *Hike!*" He stepped back quickly. Everything seemed to be in slow motion again.

The commentator shouted, "I can't believe they are trying this!"

Alex took off running to the left side of the field. All of the Dolphins' defensive players shifted in Alex's direction, knowing he would try to make a run for it. It was the final play of the game, and the clock was winding down with seven seconds left. Alex turned right and threw the ball to the right side of the field before he crossed the line of scrimmage on the left side. He had tricked the defense into thinking he was going to run for it, and they had left Tommy Thomas wide open. Thomas caught the ball, stepped into the end zone, and held the ball up in the air.

"And it's good!" yelled Troy.

"That was incredible!" Chuck shouted.

Everyone in the stadium who was a Lions fan stood up and celebrated loudly. Alex began moving his hands and arms like he was cocking and shooting an assault rifle, like some happy, immature kid. There were two seconds left on the clock. The score was 35–34, and the Lions were now in the lead. The Dolphins would have one opportunity to run the ball back at the kickoff, but it did not happen. The Super Bowl game was over! Many rich people from high places, people with cameras, players, and others ran on to the huge football field to celebrate the victory. Alex Revere was the main target.

Different people with microphones gathered around Alex. He spoke a few words concerning the victory. He was later awarded the Super Bowl MVP award. The twenty-year-old rookie wiped his eyes, put on his football cap, and spoke at the podium.

"First of all, I thank God today for helping me win this trophy," he said, holding it up. "I must say. It feels good to be the first rookie quarterback in the history of the NFL to win the Super Bowl. It felt good to break some of the most amazing records. But it really hurts me that my granny passed away a few days ago and didn't get to see me play in this game today. I'm going to miss her dearly.

"I want to thank my fans who didn't turn their backs on me when the false domestic violence charges were brought against me. I really appreciate that. Um, I must thank my coach, because he's motivated me to accomplish each and every game all the way up to today. And, most of all, I want to thank Tom Brady," Alex said. He paused for a second. "If the greatest quarterback ever, is here today, I need him to come forward, please. I have a gift for him," Alex said.

Brady was, indeed, present at the Super Bowl and came forward. Due to his greatness, he was allowed to come up on the stage where all of the high officials and winning players were. As Tom was walking up, Alex held up the 2017 number 12 New England Patriots missing Super Bowl jersey. "My granny bought me this jersey for my birthday two-and-a-half years ago. Someone sold it to her for a little over seven hundred thousand dollars. This is your jersey that came up missing after you made a miraculous comeback against the Atlanta Falcons in Super Bowl 51. I've worn it under my jersey during all my high school, college, and NFL games, and I've never lost a game with it on. But today … today I want to give it back to you, man!" said Alex, smiling. He handed the jersey back to its rightful owner. Tom held it up to examine.

Thanks, Alex! I've searched all over the world for this jersey," said the great quarterback.

Everybody in the stadium and on the stage began clapping their hands. Brady and Revere shook hands and embraced one another. Afterward, Alex stepped forward to the podium and spoke again. "Also, I must tell everyone that I've decided to retire after this one year. I've decided I'm leaving the NFL. I want to go back to college and get my bachelor's and doctorate degrees. Thank you all!" he said, smiling.

Everyone began clapping their hands once more. Two people in the bleachers spoke to one another concerning Alex returning the jersey. "What a damn fool! I would have kept that lucky jersey," said an old drunken man.

"Ya damn right! I would've kept it and won four more rings!" said the other old drunk man.

The NFL commissioner stepped forward, shook Alex's hand and spoke. "Congratulations, Alex Revere! Well done, son! Regardless, you won all of your games fair and square."

Later that year, Alex was surprised to hear that a new movie had been released about him and the missing Super Bowl jersey. Millions of people had purchased his <u>Revere</u> number 15 jersey for a little over a hundred dollars. He smiled as he looked online and saw that the new film had raked in an enormous amount of money. Alex looked on a shelf and saw a picture of him and his deceased granny on his eighteenth birthday, laughing together. Alex grabbed the photo and kissed the woman he missed the most. "Thank you, Granny, for buying me Tom's missing Super Bowl jersey," he said, smiling.

Printed in the United States
by Baker & Taylor Publisher Services